Seriously. Thank-you for buying this book. The magnificent, paper-based object you currently hold in your hand is a celebration of the printed word. The pages are crisp and pristine, just waiting for you to crack the spine and get started. Are you a corner folder or a strict book mark-ist? Will you scribble your inspired notes in the margins, or will you stick to the blank notes in the back? Or maybe you won't write in it at all save for your name neatly printed in the front. Whether you read this book once, promptly turning it over to a thrift store, or you make it a permanent fixture in your personal library, we salute you for buying this book and for supporting the author who wrote it.

Dora Mae Productions is a small outfit flying by the seat of its pants in NYC. We're a progressive group of writers and artists trying to get our work out there to readers like you. We're interested in your feedback. Seriously. And if you know anybody in the film industry (especially Clint Eastwood), we think each one of these stories would translate to the screen.

But first, we want you to read this book and love it. We're not into this whole-unrequited-love-thing. We experienced enough of that in high school, thank-you very much. So read on and squeeze as much pleasure as you can out of this book. We hope you two have a long and meaningful relationship.

Dora Mae Productions

www.doramae.com

Praise for

Tales of Wonder from the Garden State

Debbie Jones has built these four stories with sweetness, suspense, sadness and a sure eye for the details of human problems, personalities and possibilities. This is a wonderful voice with a wide range of detailed imagining and it will keep you turning the pages with fascination and joy.

Anne McCormick - Trustee - Merton Legacy Trust

Jones' lonely, isolated characters hang between this world and the next. I'm tempted to call these stories supernatural suspense, but the characters are too fine, too empathic. Deborah Jones' hallucinatory, dream-like stories deserve a wider audience.

David Johnston - Playwright - *Candy & Dorothy, Busted Jesus Comix*

Debbie Jones' stories sing. Their music is life as we all know it – we recognize each other and ourselves – at times tough, other times gentle, but always her characters wage the human struggle to assert their self-respect and dignity. Do not miss reading these songs.

Fred Jerome - Author - *The Einstein Files*

The writing in these stories is imaginative, exciting and beautiful to read. They are mystical and sometimes violent. The words of Debbie Jones are haunting. Things are kept from the reader; I had to keep reading to find out what would become of the characters I had become so involved with. These are stories that need and deserve an audience.

Elaine J. Schwartz - Director - The Center School

On #6:

The style of the author winds its way into the mind of the reader with word pictures that will bring a smile to every father who has ever tossed a baseball with their child. One can all but smell the pungent odor of White Owl cigars, the aroma of a Ballantine beer and hear the voice of Mel Allen rising from a radio. It is the magical work of a person in love with a game that does and will always transcend each generation.

Pete Foley - baseball aficionado

Step into Debbie Jones' world and you will want to stay a long while. Set in mystic communities strung along the Northeastern seaboard of the U.S., populated by characters just off-kilter enough to fascinate, her yarns are finely spun gossamer. From the adventurous child to the elderly dreamer, while verbalizing Jones' excellent ear for regional patois, these people carry the reader along on journeys of mystery and wonder but, Jones is not one for neat bow-tying. Each story is a journey for the thinking person.

Judith Katz-Schwartz - Author - *Protecting Your Collectible Treasures: Secrets of a Collecting Diva* - TV Personality, Actress

Plays by Debbie Jones

My Type

Stripper's Prayer

The Breezeway

Jeremy Rudge

My Boy Bill

Noah's Arc

The Marlboro Woman

The Last Christmas Party (feature film)

Tales of Wonder from the Garden State

by Debbie Jones

drawings by Rebecca Lally

Dora Mae Productions • New York

Dora Mae Productions • New York

For information, visit www.talesofwonderfromthegardenstate.com

Dora Mae Productions LLC
Post Office Box 141
Planetarium Station
N.Y., N.Y. 10024-0141
www.doramae.com

ISBN 978-0-615-41772-1

For Marie Quinlan and Fred Jones
gone now but forever my undying gratitude for a childhood
well-spent

TALES

INTRODUCTION

Great writers -- no, I want to stay away from those words: those words put together sound dead, and the thing about writers who stay in you and stick with you is that they keep leaping about inside you and they're not dead at all - so: writers who stay in you and stick with you make their place your own.   And Debbie Jones' place is New Jersey. Small towns in New Jersey, it would seem. She's also demonstrated this in her thrilling play *The Breezeway*; although she's demonstrated in another beautiful play, *Jeremy Rudge*, that her place is clearly the Ozarks or someplace like it, so I should maybe not just assume that New Jersey is her place. I think she could convince me that Singapore is her place if she wrote about it.   But let's stick with New Jersey, where these astonishing stories are set. And I mean that word: astonishing. Because what Debbie Jones does in these stories is a thing I can't exactly recall another writer doing. She makes the supernatural natural. She makes it earthy. Some writers make it whimsically everyday in its feeling, many make it weird and permanently haunting. Debbie Jones makes it earthy. She makes it as earthy as she makes the everyday texture of life, which she does wonderfully. And so the texture of the everyday life in these stories and the advent of the supernatural into them is seamless. You feel it with a little jolt and shock but you feel it naturally.   It can happen in a sand pit, in the parking lot of a small town at night from the back seat of a car, in the yard of a beautiful young woman in a fieldstone house at the edge of another small town. You can feel it in Yankee Stadium (the old one). You can feel it from a loving dog. Every one of these stories is a thrilling trip. I hope you take these trips. New Jersey will never be the same. Neither will your life.

Austin Pendleton – playwright, director, actor

Blackie

Blackie

There were lots of interesting things in the dump pit but the pump worked. It was rusty brown with a big lip. It took awhile - longer and longer in the even years of her childhood - but if you pumped it just right - the handle was squiggly - the pump yielded water. It was the clearest water she'd ever seen - clear in the sunlight - clear in the cloudy. She thought it was sort of magic - the way the old pump stood there in the weeds pouring forth. She wondered about the water too and where it came from. She'd asked a Farmer once. Their names were Farmer and they were farmers too. They grew corn in summer and raised stock and slaughtered it and brought it to market. They cut out sides of beef for the community and kept it there on their land underground in a chilling well. She'd seen it a few times with her Mother. It was under some floorboards in their barn. It had a big hook on a chain up over it and when you looked down, it was deep enough to be dark.

The Farmer said the old pump used to be for livestock. He said probably there'd been a watershed or just a wash for cows before there was a dump in that pit. He said there were underground springs that ran up cold out of the ground and underground rivers too. That sounded thrilling to her. She'd try to imagine an underground river churning and turning through darkened banks and unlit skies. The brown pump was all there was to help her in her imaginings. It came from another time. Everything about what had been before she got here seemed good to her. Little things stood as reminders of then - like the pump or a hitching post or the cobalt blue glass discarded in the trough by the railroad tracks. It was changing now. This town of hers was changing. The nineteenth century was sitting fallow on the fields of the twentieth century waiting to be gone. She felt it - shifting time. All the children could feel it. It was in the light. They'd been born in-between.

The part she liked the most was when the water finished gurgling up and shot out of the rusty lip in a clean hard wave. She'd put her hand in it and feel the difference with her fingers. It wasn't like air. It was cold and sweet. She'd bring her mouth to it and suck it off her fingers. Bits of it would catch in the sun and look like glint or land in her brown hair and sparkle there for a minute. She liked getting a drink from the old rusty pump as much as any cow she'd bet. She liked its secrecy for nobody she knew used the pump anymore except kids. It was hidden from view in a shoot of weeds. Sometimes when she was out there, Blackie would come all wired up and tense and want a mouthful and she'd slow down the flow so the poor mutt could get his tongue around it. Blackie ran around her town her whole childhood with nobody to take him over. Her Mother said he was just too wild. All the kids she knew gave him leftover lunches and Hostess cupcakes and sometimes liver. In the Spring there'd be puppies on the blocks that had one white ear and the rest all black and one of the Fathers would get a shotgun down and try to shoot Blackie but all the kids would know and come running and then the Father would have to stop it or kill one of the kids.

In the Fall, Blackie'd be gone. That was strange too. Sometimes she wondered where he went in the Indian summers. But then in the Spring, he'd be all around the place again. She never had a dog of her own. Her Mother didn't want a pet. They'd got a kitten once. One of the farm cats had a litter. But the kitten they got became a cat that climbed her Mother's drapes and peed on the rug behind the sofa. Her Mother kept locking the kitten up in the garage when she went to the store or someplace. And that got the cat wilder and more certain of getting away, so in the nights, he'd sneak out of an open window or through the garage door when her Father came in, and he'd fight it out with the marmalade tom from the other block. She'd hear Kitty-puss in the night yowling. And that made her Mother mad too. But Kitty-puss had nothing to stay home about and it got so the only lap he'd come to was hers because he knew she wouldn't lock him in the garage. And then one early morning in July that was already hot enough for a good swim, Kitty-puss didn't come home his usual way climbing up the roses to the roof and sneaking through her screen which she always left unlatched. And she looked and looked for him calling out. And pretty soon all the local kids were calling out "Kitty-puss! Kitty-puss! Come back!" until her Mother couldn't stand it anymore and came out of the house and found the cat underneath the pickup truck next door. They all got on their stomachs and looked under. The macadam was hot on her face. Kitty-puss wasn't twitching his tail the way he did when he wanted kids to stay away. She could see his eyes though. Green gleam in the dark. No purring. No sound. It made her scared seeing Kitty-puss still like that. She wouldn't crawl under so her Mother did. Her Mother had a dress on and socks and an apron. She'd been cleaning. Her knee got scratched on the tiny pebbles that were under there. She had grease or oil on her elbow too. She dragged Kitty-puss out by his tail. The cat was stiff and had flies in its bloody ear.

They buried it in the garden by the forsythia. It was a mound. Her Mother stood beside her with a spade. They were both sweating. Her Dad wasn't home yet from the city. Her little brother stood off aways watching her real hard. Some of the local kids were in the lilacs. She thought a long time about that cat while she was standing there. She decided she would never be any trouble to someone. She decided she would never have a cat. But then later when she was on the toilet in the cooler months of September, then October, she'd look out the bathroom window to the mound in the garden and think of him. She watched the rains that came in the Fall and the snow that fell in Winter erase the mound from her Mother's garden and in April, when it was smooth there and even with the rest of the topsoil, she decided that cat was gone.

Maybe that's why she liked Blackie. It didn't matter how much trouble he was, nobody could ever get him. She also liked it that he came up to her. It made her distinct. Blackie avoided human contact even with kids. He'd fool around skirting them, herding them, in and out, around and around. And every time she got out to the old pump in the dump pit, just when she'd get the water going, Blackie'd be there. He had a long red tongue. He'd wait for her to get some water, then he'd come up alongside and lap some too. Then when she'd follow the old footpaths out through the fields into the trees, she'd catch glimpses of Blackie escaping out into a clearing or running under the fir trees or waiting on a rise just ahead. It was like he knew where she was going before she did. It was like Blackie was her dog.

When she'd turned eleven, it was decided in her house by her Mother she could go off the blocks. There were only two blocks at their end of town. The land between the depot and her street was filled with open fields. Hers was the next to the last street. This decision of her Mother's came as a big relief. She'd been wanting to bust out of the confines of those two blocks for a long time because one Friday after supper before she was allowed, the boy up the block who was fourteen got her to cross the Boulevard into the old apple orchard. He wanted to show her the tunnel he'd dug with some other boys. It was deep and it went under the street. She knew about it. All the kids knew about it. But none of the girls had seen where it was. Not so far as she knew.

She looked back down her block. She couldn't see her house from the corner because of 2 big fir trees on the property next up. Somehow not being able to see her Mother's house made it possible to do. She tried to make it look like nothing going against her Mother but her saddle shoes hitting that macadam felt like slivers of light shooting up out of the ground. He pulled her into the orchard fast. She couldn't see very well. All the branches were down low and kept hitting her in the face. Nobody cared about these trees anymore. She used to stand at the end of her block and wonder if they minded being like all the other trees - just there with nobody to pick them. He yelled out to her to stop! Then she saw why. They'd put evergreen branches across the hole they'd dug down to the entrance of the tunnel. The boy who was fourteen dragged them off and jumped in. The hole was up to his neck. Then he did a funny thing - he put a hand up to help her down - help her down?! His hand had a deep cut under a flap of skin on the thumb. His fingernails were all bloody and raggedy. It was like he was proud of his hands - nicked and cut. They didn't look like boys' hands at all. This boy was the first leader of men she would meet. She wouldn't have put it that way then. She would have said he was distinct - that there was something about him that held him out from other kids. He wasn't afraid of regular stuff and the stuff that did scare him, he made a joke out of and busted through. Inside she felt like him - she felt like busting through - like making a joke and busting through. And here he was giving her her chance. She jumped down in. He told her he wanted her to see the insides. He said they'd gotten almost all the way across the Boulevard underneath but that they hadn't started back up on the other side yet. She could see it in his eyes - he really wanted her to see it. There was a tunnel dug under the Boulevard that nobody knew about but kids. It was really something. He told her to get on her belly and crawl. When he said belly, she felt funny and covered hers up. He said "come'awn. " She looked back down her block. It looked far off across the Boulevard all of a sudden to her - almost like another town. He said "Ya' scared?" She wasn't scared - not of crawling in the tunnel. She was excited was what she was. She wanted to squeeze into that hole and crawl through the dirt and see. But she knew when she got home, she'd have to say how she got the dirt all over her Ship n' Shore blouse and she knew she couldn't lie and if she told the truth, her Father and the other fathers would find the tunnel and fill it up. "See, it's easy. " He was halfway in looking back at her. It wasn't any good. She couldn't tell him why. She just climbed up out of the pit and pushed her way through the apple branches and ran across the Boulevard without looking back.

There were other times like that when she wanted to go do something but then she didn't. That's why when her Mother said she could go off the blocks, she never told her Mother or anybody where she went. There was a safety in that. She wasn't breaking rules. There were no rules for off the blocks. They never talked about it. She didn't know exactly why. Usually, her Mother liked to talk about stuff - like holding on with both hands to her bicycle bars - like not playing in the Cleary's garage - like coming inside when it got dark out. And her Mother always had an awful story to go with her rules about some kid who did what he shouldn't and got paralyzed or lost a foot. Maybe it was because her Mother wasn't home so much now that she was allowed off the block. Maybe that's how come they never got around to the rules for off the block. No time to talk. She hated rules. There were so many of them. A girl had to hold herself in check and think 'Now is this against the rules?' Now that she could, she went and she didn't look for rules in the trees or on the hills or under rocks. She'd just go and go. There was no lie for her in not lying and since nobody knew where she went, they never asked and she didn't need to tell them.

That summer she was eleven she learned to grab the rocks with her toes and find dirt instead of thorns with the bottom of her feet. The trees thickened into woods and then the ground swelled up. She climbed with ease in her barefeet. She loved climbing. The higher she went, the steeper it got so she'd have to pull on saplings and the edges of rocks but she'd get there. There was a slide of water that ran across pure rock and then on down the mountain. It was only a couple of inches deep. But it rippled and rushed and was ice blue on her red cold ankles. She never did find out where it came from. Her conscience kept her in town limits. She didn't cross the county road that was on the other side and halfway down the mountain. Nor did she follow the old jeep pass that was off to the left and led right through that string of the Ramapos. The jeep pass was jutty and water glistened in the tire tracks after a rain - red muddy water that held the reflection of the sky. There were bears up there but she was a sensible country child. She looked out for stray cubs. She wouldn't make a mama bear mad for anything. And if there was a papa bear coming down the mountain into town, the siren would blast and she'd run home like a normal child and stay inside looking out all the windows with her little brother hoping to see the bear.

Blackie was usually along. He'd stand on the jeep track with his tongue out waiting for her to follow. She figured it must be where he lived - somewhere in those hills. Indian Summer looked beautiful up through those hills. Sometimes she'd stand there and look for a long time. But then she'd say 'nah - not today, Blackie' - and continue on. More often than not, he followed her up the big hill that backed their town. When they got to the part that went straight up - it was only the last twenty feet of the climb - Blackie'd stop and watch her go. He couldn't get up there. Once she constructed a big sling out of old towels her Father had in the garage. She thought it up nights watching the leafy shadows play on the ceiling in the dark of her room. She got some rope and doubled up the towels and made her Mother sew it together just like she wanted on the Singer sewing machine. She told her Mother it was a doll hammock and it would be some of the time. She tried the hardest she ever tried to get Blackie to get in that sling so then she could lug him to the top of the mountain. But he wouldn't do it.

On the top of the mountain was the smooth part - it was the smoothest part she'd ever know. There was honey-colored grass that was softer than a mattress and it bent over in the breeze that was always up there. The softest breeze touched her hair and made each single blade of honey grass bend. It smelled like the valley - like the pastures, and the lowland by the river, and the far-off green. There were trees - not a lot - young trees not much more than saplings that stood in a small bunch at one end of the honey-colored grass. That was all. That and the tops of grey rocks like the backs of buffaloes. But in the smooth part grew the thickest honey-colored grass. She loved that - being alone up there.

It took a long time to get up but when she did, she felt like she was the first one who ever did it. Every time - she felt like she was the first one. She'd sit down in the honey-colored grass and feel in her bones she was the first one. She knew at eleven that wasn't possible. She wasn't a fool. But still she felt it. She knew other kids in that town in other times must have made this climb - maybe grownups too though a grownup wouldn't have a reason for coming up here. There was nothing to do up here but look. The city was far off to the east poking up into the sky like a magic purple shadow. Behind her to the west was a factory that let out ugly green smoke. It didn't belong in this place. Her Father said it was a sign of things to come. So she'd pretend it wasn't there. Sometimes, when she was looking, she felt like she was looking at human memory - that what was out there had been there for a long time - not all of it - but most of it. And it was changing. She felt it most up here - the changing. A part of her wanted to make it stop. She wouldn't mind being eleven forever if she could make it stop.

On one day, she fell asleep up there - tired out from the climb and when she woke up, it was close to sunset. The climb up was 2 hours - the climb down was faster - maybe an hour and a half but she knew she'd missed supper and that her Mother had already gotten the whole block out looking for her. She had to get home. And she had to do it fast.

Blackie was barking down below. She looked over and could see him underneath the trees. He wasn't in the usual spot waiting for her to climb back down. He was running off to the east - the opposite of the way she'd come up. And he was barking. She figured it must have been his barking that woke her. The sunset was beautiful. It was long and pink with purple streaks. The breeze on her face was hard. She held her hair back. She was glad she was seeing it this way now because she knew by nightfall, she'd be in the worst trouble of her life. She'd have to go inside her self and not come out for a long time. Her house would be quiet with no words for her. There weren't many words just for her as it was, but now there'd be harsh words and angry eyes and trust would be gone. And unless she turned a liar, there'd be rules for off the block. People thought she didn't care when they were mad at her. They thought they needed to be mean to her to make her understand how mad they were. But they didn't need to be mean. It hurt her so much she couldn't understand how they could be doing it. All they had to do was tell her not to do it again. But instead her Mother made her Father get angry at her. It was at every meal. She felt like a nail getting driven into a beam of wood. They would never stop. And then she'd have to tell it all to the priest in confession and he'd tell her she was bad and she couldn't stand it. She couldn't stand it - them calling her bad. She wasn't bad. She was good. She was always proving to them how good she was. But nobody ever saw it. Not one person ever saw it. The sun was a pink ball. It was dropping into the horizon. She turned.

Blackie was there like a ghost in the fading light at the east end of the smooth place. He was watching her with his head cocked. So he could get up here by himself, could he. She watched him paw the ground. She figured he wanted her to follow him. And she was right because when she did, he ran ahead. On the eastern side of the smooth place, there was a path down. It was steep but not like the other side. It didn't even look like a path but it was there. Yellow grass grew up between the rocks and she was able to climb her way down. The light was disappearing fast. There were red shadows across the rocks now and in the tops of the trees. The breeze was blowing harder than she'd ever felt it. Blackie panted along up ahead holding himself up now and then to make sure she was with him. This was probably faster down - now that she thought about it. She'd never approached the mountain from this side. It was up at the far end beyond the streets at the place where the Boulevard left town. She could say she was sorry - she lost track of time. She wouldn't have to say where'd she'd been. She could say she was up at the far end of town fooling around and that was no lie. They'd still be mad but not as mad as they'd be if they knew she was on top of the biggest hill in town all by herself with no buddy.

She was back on the ridge - firmer footing - and still Blackie led her on down across more rockfaces but nowhere was it as steep as the other side. She'd remember this. It was plain easier. They were in the trees now going down. She had to grab hold here and there but not much. Then it was darker all of a sudden and the trees were like shadows and the shadows were in the millions. It was beautiful to her and scary in the dark. She started running down now. She could feel her barefeet slapping at dirt - closer now to the valley. Blackie was barking and hollering and herding her all of a sudden. She had no choice. She had to stop.

Through the trees there was free wide open sky. She could see it. She reached and pushed aside a branch and could see nothing but thin air. She looked down. It was the old sandpit. Boy oh boy, she'd heard about this. She'd heard stories. The drop was a couple of houses high. More. The pink in the sunset was riding the ridge of the sandpit halfway around but straight down it was deep and dark. She knew what was down there alright. Water straight down. It was bottomless. All the mothers said - not just hers. The sandpit company had hit a natural underground spring and it had spit up into the sandpit like an oil well and filled it with the coldest water there was around here. She knew this because the boy who was fourteen said so and so did his brother and all their friends. Those boys went swimming here. They weren't supposed to - it wasn't allowed - everybody said so - even the police. But they did it just the same. She longed for such freedom. She figured the cold water must be coming from the same place as the water that came out of the old pump. Looking down at it was like looking at another time - like it had secrets. It was to her as if the dark water in the sandpit knew things about time she'd never know. The water in the sand pit knew about yearning and how much she needed to grow up and be free.

She watched a boy named Ralph get whipped by the pointer stick on his behind. The priest whipped him and whipped him. The

11

pointer stick made a whizzing through her ears. She couldn't stand it. It sounded like wasps coming after her brother in the June he was 3. She got all hot hearing the whipping. She put the heels of her hands in her ears and she didn't look. But then in the classroom, the air stood still. The minutest particles hung still in the sunlight before her eyes and it was over like a bang. But there was no bang. But it was over. Once and forever over. Not just the whipping but the mad. The priest smiled at Ralph. He put the pointer stick back in the chalk rack. He told Ralph he could return to his seat and when Ralph did, the priest watched him get there. He had a look of respect in his eyes for Ralph taking it like he did. If Ralph had hollered out, it would have been okay or better somehow - for her. But he didn't. He was silent during the whipping. And the priest thought that was good. The mad grownups felt for girls never got over. It just hung in the air forever on and on and always hurt because it could never, ever be over. That was one big difference between girls and boys. Nobody ever stopped being mad at girls.

There was a story for the sandpit:

> There was a boy who didn't have a Mother. His name was Butch. He liked to grab the lid off the neighbor woman's garbage can. He pretended it was a shield or something. Butch was a wild boy. One day in the hot August heat, there was nothing to do but pray - that's what the neighbor woman said to his Dad from her front porch to his through the trellises. "There's nuthin' to do but pray." Butch's Dad had a quart bottle of Schlitz behind the ramblers and 3 more in the ice box. Butch had a full quart of beer before he took off that day. His Dad found it missing later. He jumped up on a rumble seat of an old black Ford parked at the corner then down off the other side. Nobody yelled at him. They'd given up. The Mothers on the block were afraid of what he'd do. Butch was a wild boy. He crossed the dogless road and went knee deep into the straw grass

with the locusts. He smashed the garbage can lid up against some low down trees that were hitting him in his face. Crabapples fell like rocks. At the end of the field, he threw one at a garage window and broke it. When he got to the top of the sandpit, he pulled at his T-shirt balling it up into armpit sweat. He dropped the garbage can lid into thin air and stepped off the ridge into the canyon. He landed perfectly squat on the lid 20 feet down and went for a long slow slide. His T-shirt he flung out ahead of him down into the ice cold cool of the wellspring and he watched it fall straight at the dark - it was coming fast - right at his chest and he licked off the sweat at the top of his lip and got ready to feel the bite of the cold and - and then right behind him, the sandpit moved. He heard it coming like a dream - a billion crystals of sand like an army of ants and he knew in his gut, he could beat it.

That's the way the story went when the boy who was fourteen told it. Her Mother had another way of telling it:

The story was that a boy who had no mother took to sliding down the great tall walls of the sandpit and one day in mid-August when the sun was hot and the air was dry, he'd been overtaken by an avalanche of sand and dirt he could not outrun on his garbage can lid. And when they found him and it took 25 men all night digging, his mouth was open wide as a scream and packed to the brim with sand crystals.

Grass weed stuck out like slick between her toes reaching for earth that wasn't there. The wind whistled up from the pit. They'd dug out the mountain and struck water and left it there like Mars. The deep walls of the sandpit slid down into the dark water at its base. With the sun set like it was, the wall at the far end cut a reflection like a wedge of cheese into the black water. And deep down into the dark reflection, the moon hung out like a lost star.

Blackie was showing her the fastest way down. He was a smart dog. All she had to do was step off the side of the mountain and slide down the biggest slide God ever made into the water and swim across it to the other side and run home through the fields. And they'd be mad but she could say she lost track of the time and was fooling around and she'd never do it again. And she'd be home in less than a half hour. She'd been off the blocks for a while now and knew about distance and what it took in her town to get from here to there. With this wind, her clothes would dry. They had to dry. If she went Blackie's way, she didn't need a single lie.

She wasn't afraid. She felt a rush inside her that she hadn't felt before. Was this what boys felt when they broke the rules? She believed she could do it. She could slide down the side of the mountain and be home in under a half hour. She thought about the boy who had no mother. She wondered if it was true and if it was, which ending was true. The other one? Or her Mother's? Could the sand on a sandpit wall form into an avalanche like snow and just bury people in it? Could it do that? Or was there a warning? Would she hear it and be able to get out of the way? Would she be dead if she did this? In a few minutes, would she be dead? Would they find her dead? And if they did, would they have a nice funeral with a white coffin and all the kids who had ever been mean to her would regret it because now they could never say they were sorry? And what if they didn't find her? Would the story of the boy who had no mother become the story of a girl who had no sense? She tried to think of how the mothers would tell it?

> There was a girl who had no sense who lived in this town and one night she went out to the hills and got lost in the dark and she couldn't see or anything and the next thing she knew, she fell off the top of the mountain straight into the old sandpit. The water there is bottomless, you know. She was never found.

She blinked in her mind. Maybe they wouldn't find out what happened to her. She'd just disappear like the town and the way it used to be. 'There used to be a water pump, and a barn, and a

The water there is bottomless, you know.

girl...who had no sense. ' It would make her Mother sad not having her. She could feel tears stinging inside her. It'd be so sad to be dead and not see her Mother or her Father or her brother anymore. She felt a tear slide down her cheek. Blackie was licking her hand.

She sat down on her bottom on the edge of the sandpit. She reached with her left foot and felt the sand. It wasn't soft like beach sand. It had pebbles in it. She dug her right heel into the sand. It held. She shifted her weight off the mountain. Blackie was panting near her ear. This was going to be okay. She just had to stop thinking so much and concentrate on what she was doing. The pink sunset on the ridge withdrew suddenly and was replaced almost right away with blue moonlight. She looked up. There it was - a big old lopsided moon. She looked down to see if it was still there in the black water but instead there was blue glow. The moon made the water shine. She could see the walls all the way down now. They curved into the black water then reflected back up to themselves in the blue glow. It was like the moon came out just for her - so she could see. This was a hard thing to do. She was higher up than a Ferris Wheel. And she thought she was afraid too. But she couldn't tell if she was afraid to do it or afraid of her Mother. These feelings were mixed up inside of her. She dug her bottom into the wall of the sandpit and sat still for a minute. Nothing happened. She could if she wanted to - turn around and go back the usual way. That's what her Mother would tell her 'Go back the usual way now. ' The blue moonlight and Blackie would help her. She'd get home alright. She didn't have to do this if she didn't want to. But there was part of her building up inside that wanted to do this. There were things she'd wanted to do since she was very little - like jumping off the roof. Or riding her two wheeler across a rafter. Or hiding under a car or in a drain well. These were things she had never done.

She let herself slide a little and as she did, she looked back up real quick. Blackie wasn't there. There was nothing there but bushes and tall trees standing in the moonlight to watch her go.

She was picking up speed so she kicked out and some pebbles to the left of her let loose and started sliding down - rolling, clicking pebbles. She rammed both feet into the sand and stopped. The rain of pebbles kept coming. Then up behind her, she heard the sand let loose. More was coming. How could this be? Sand and pebbles raced past splashing her left side showering her with dirt and dust. She had to cough and cough. Then it was all past her rolling down the sandpit. For a minute, she sat there listening to it go. She could hear it pinging down. The sound kept getting further and further off. Then after what seemed to her a long time, the plipping and plopping came back up like a crackle as each pebble hit the wellspring one by one and disappeared inside.

It was quiet in the sandpit - waiting quiet. So quiet. Then the wind came up and blew the softest whistle in her ear.

How could it be? How could it be that the only time in her life she decided to do exactly what she wanted, she got paid back - 'in spades' her Father would say. How come the boy who was fourteen got to climb up to the top of a pine that wouldn't hold him and sneak in through somebody's broken cellar window and take one of the Farmer's tractors for a ride and never got caught at it - not once? And here she was on the side of the sandpit getting run down by an avalanche on her first try!

Mad now, she yelled out for Blackie. "Blackie!"

All that came back at her was her own voice yelling "-lack-y!"

It felt like somebody was making fun of her. It felt like somebody was trying to scare her. She decided she wanted somebody up there with her - some kid - a state trooper - her Dad. She decided she really was the girl who had no sense. She decided she was the girl who didn't trust her Mother. Mothers knew about stuff like this. They knew how to keep their children out of harm's way. That's what her Grandmother called it - Harm's Way. Like it was a town or place on earth or somebody's street. She didn't want to be a chicken girl. But she knew the sand around her was disturbed. And she knew very well that sand is a substance that blows with the wind. And she knew in her heart that what her Mother said about the motherless boy was true. That one night in another time before this place of hers decided to change, there was a boy who drowned in sand.

She decided to turn over on her stomach and crawl back up to the top but when she did, the sand underneath her slid in a great big chunk down and she was stretched out wide on it sliding down the wall of the sandpit with it. And there was nothing she could do but not swallow.

Then it stopped.

The sound of the sandpit when it stopped was like the earth standing still. Nothing breathed or moved. She pictured the spaceman in *The Day The Earth Stood Still* giving orders to the earth men. She remembered the sand that sucked the boy and his whole town into the earth in *Invaders From Mars*. Maybe she deserved what she got. Maybe that was the whole thing. Maybe girls with no sense just deserved what they got. She thought of white sheets snapping in the wind on her Mother's clothesline and the tops of birch trees silver in the air. She thought of the sandpit and how it moved. It moved like an animal under her - it moved like a million ants.

She turned over on her back with her palms flat underneath her. The wind blew some more sand in her mouth. She spit. She could see the moon. A cloud was coming to cover it. In a minute she'd be in the dark. She pulled out her hands then stretched her arms out as far as she could. Nothing bad happened. She decided to inch her way down on her back. She decided to keep her weight even. She did this because it worked on ice that time one of the kids fell through. They'd all done it together. There'd been no choice. There was no grownup. The boy who was fourteen led them through it - a line of kids with their bodies spread out even holding onto each other's ankles til' the smallest one - a girl named Carole - reached the girl who was in the freezing cold water. After that, the boy who was fourteen was treated better by all the mothers even though the girl in the freezing cold water lost her little toe. It was in a jar at the doctor's office. It was black. It was a warning to all kids.

The cloud came and so did the dark. She wondered if now one of the fathers would kill Blackie. That somehow they'd know Blackie was the one to get her into this. She wondered how come Blackie did it. How come Blackie led her here? And where was he? She started moving first her feet, then her bottom, then her shoulders slowly down. Rocks cut into her back. It didn't hurt exactly. Feet, bottom, shoulders, move along, girl. After each set, she'd stop and wait for something bad to happen - for some sound. When nothing came but the wind, she'd move along down - feet, bottom, shoulders - never mind if she was getting cut. Then she slid several feet down all at once - she couldn't help it - and her feet landed on something hard and stopped her like a boing on the wall of the sandpit.

She waited for sandslide but all she heard was a few pebbles plop into the water below. The water sounded closer. The wind wasn't so strong down here. She could look almost straight out at the highway now which was far off down by the river. A single set of headlights came up over the hill in a fog then focused down on the road like sweepers and ran across her eyes until they were gone. She was on a ledge of hard dirt. She could feel it with her toes.

She thought about Brigadoon. It was the first show she ever saw. Her cousin was the star. He played Tommy Albright in his high school production. She thought about mysterious things she'd never know the answer to - like the lady down the block who never came out of her house. She was from the other time and so was her house. It sat close to the road. Her Mother told her in Revolutionary times, they did that. They kept the houses close to the roads. So they could see what was coming. There weren't any cars then - just horses galloping in the night. There wasn't electricity - just candles in the windows. Her Mother put electric candles in their windows at Christmas. People missed candles.

19

People missed a lot of things they'd never see again - like upside-down pineapple cakes and homemade taffy. She didn't like cooked pineapples and her Mother hated the mess of pulling taffy. She thought about swimming and how much she liked it. She thought about her little brother who was always in trouble. He did things he shouldn't all the time. He set fires and threw bricks. Then he hid under the bed. He was a continuously curious boy who wanted to see what would happen. He was looking for answers too. Well she could tell him something about this if she ever saw him again.

She felt herself going down. The chunk of dirt under her feet was dropping off under her weight. It was slow at first. She tried turning over - grabbing her fingers into the dirt. But she couldn't get all the way over and fell back on her back and then slid sideways - her body moving around clockwise. Then there were rocks cutting into the back of her scalp. It hurt. And then she felt her legs coming up over her head and she did a backwards somersault and then another one and then for a split second, she was out in thin air reaching for the wall of the sandpit and then her left knee jammed down into rock and she was feeling awful pain and she was on her side rolling and rolling the fastest she ever rolled down any hill in her life and the black kept getting bigger and bigger and then she rolled off the sandpit wall entirely backwards into thin air! And it was so quiet looking upwards at the moon with one star off to the right. The cloud was gone. And then she hit the hard black water and sunk down into it.

The cold made her come to. It was shocking it was so cold. And she'd felt cold water before - up at Cape Cod in June with her family. Nobody - not even a kid - could stand that cold water more than five minutes. It was that cold. And blue. The moon made it electric in the black water. Blue moonlight shone all around her. She could see her white hands spread out like pale crabs floating down and down. It truly was bottomless. It was a bottomless pit leading down to a secret underground river. She'd get to see where the pump water came from. All the reflections. The unlit sky. She'd ride and ride down the splashing cold underground river and come out where?

She heard something. She waited for it to come again. It was a tune - an underwater tune. Sometimes her friend, Janet, would go underwater with her and they'd yell words at each other and then they'd come up and see if they knew what each other said. Underwater sounds sounded loud but stuck - like an echo stopped in mid-air. It was an underwater tune - one somebody made up - a kid's tune.

There was a boy down there in the dark with only a smile in his mouth. She was pretty sure it was a boy. He looked so far down. Everything was clear and cold. He was kicking his feet out like a silent slow snow angel riding up in the blue dark. The boy was a free creature. All he had was a smile in his mouth. She wanted to breathe. She wanted to suck in one long breath and breathe. But something inside her was turning around.

The blue light was disappearing. She tried to catch it in her hands but it slipped upwards out of her reach. At the top, she could see the moon through the cold water. It let down singular shafts of blue light into the black water but she couldn't get her fingers to reach it. She felt funny. The boy below her looked pale like a jelly fish. And only a smile in his mouth. She thought she knew him - seen him before. Or maybe she dreamed him up. 'You must have dreamed that one up. ' That's what her Mother said sometimes. She could never tell why her Mother said that. Didn't her Mother see all the things she could see? Didn't her Mother know what was true?!

Just one breath.

She felt a tug - it was on her right ankle. The boy was down there holding onto her ankle. He still seemed a long way down but she was glad he got here. She watched him below her treading water - his hands and feet were going good. He was a good swimmer - that boy. She could hear his tune. She knew she could

He was a bad boy...He was a motherless boy.

sing it. It was simple. The kind of tune that got stuck in a person's head right away - like a jump-rope song.

She stopped in mid-water - black and alone.

The boy swam up to her face. He was suspended in the black water right in front of her. And all he had was a smile in his mouth. He cocked his head down. Then he did a flipover. He was a clown upside-down with his barefeet sticking out of the ends of his pants. And then she couldn't tell who was upside-down. Him or her?

She croaked. She couldn't help it. It was funny. She croaked and an explosion of bubbles came out of her mouth and rose up free in the great dark.

The boy floated up upside-down. He stopped at her face. He was right there treading water. His arms were out. She couldn't tell who was right side up. It was like they were two parts of a pinwheel waiting to blow. She could touch his face if she wanted but she didn't because there was an ant coming out from in between his lips. It was working so hard - first its little feelers then its little black bulbhead popped out. The boy held his smile real tight in his mouth but it was no use because another ant was squeezing out the corner of his lips. Then the first ant was out and floating up, and directly behind it was another ant and then another ant popping out and up. And then out of both sides of his smile came more black ants. Instead of bubbles, there were ants. And then 2 lines of ants coming one after another out the boy's nostrils. Black bubbles.

Just one breath.

She kicked out and got a full measure up before the boy got hold of her right ankle again. He was kidding around. She kicked down at him to let go and then his undershirt was on her back and in her hair. It was everywhere and she couldn't get untangled. She felt her neck jerk. Her body was awful cold. She kicked and kicked and then the boy was swimming up inside the undershirt with her - he was in there with her. And all he had was ants in his mouth. Just breathe. He put the palm of his left hand over her mouth and held it tightly there. Then he took the two main fingers of his right hand and inserted them into her nose.

He was a bad boy.

Her head was pounding and there were little tiny air needles everywhere piercing her mind like millions of silverfish swimming straight at the moon. He was a motherless boy.

She could see the moon through the hole at the top of the undershirt. She was climbing up for it and she got to it and she pulled through it and still he held onto her mouth and his fingers grew longer inside her nose. And then there was an ant crawling down from his shoulder to his arm. She watched it. It was a scout ant. It was coming for her. And she knew when it got to her, it would be bad. She lifted up her knees and struck out with both feet but when they hit the boy, it was like gooey sponge. Her feet went right through him. Was he crazy? She slid right through him and down and down into the black water.

And then the moon in the water above smashed into a million stars - like fireworks, it filled the dark with lights. And she was swimming through it like a rocket shooting up through the million dazzling diamonds straight up through the surface to the moon!

She breathed. And breathed. And breathed. The moon was shining down. She could hear the echo of her breathing. She could feel the blue pale reflection of the moon on the black water. She breathed and she breathed. And then she screamed and screamed inside her head. She was trying to yell out. Her ears crackled then opened up. Her yelling echoed and came back at her and traveled all around the walls of the sandpit - exploding like the force of time. And then not just screaming but barking and barking. She stopped herself. The barking was bouncing all over.

Blackie was swimming and swimming around her in a tight circle. He was trying to save her! Dear dog! Dear dog Blackie! She tried to grab him but he was herding her - doggy paddling her across the expanse of the wellspring to the shore. He was forcing her. There was a streetlight there - off on the Boulevard. She started swimming for it - cutting through the black water - keeping her breath as best she could. Blackie was in back of her, then to the side of her. He kept turning in the water like he was looking for something. She thought of the bad boy while she was swimming. 'You musta' dreamed that one up. ' Well, maybe she did. It didn't matter now. She was swimming. Her heart was pounding. She was a good swimmer.

Blackie was barking. She heard him now behind her. She turned around in the water and looked at the big blue pale of light reflecting in the center of the black. There was nothing there - nothing to bark at.

Then she heard it. It was so clear. Of all the things that happened in that night, his words were the clearest.

"You fuckin' piece of shit dog."

The black surface of the water didn't move - not a ripple. She was treading water - afraid to move. Could she swim better than him? Faster? Was she faster than the motherless boy?

She dug her right arm down into the black like a knife and then her left and then her right and her left and she ripped her chest free. She was riding high - swimming like a maniac. She could feel herself getting there - sense it. She could see the streetlight through the water - she kept it there in sight and swam for it. Then her feet were under her and she was stumbling out of the water and making a break for hard land.

"Blackie?!" She yelled it out.

The water in the sandpit looked so wide to her. And the moon at the top of the sandpit walls looked so high.

"-lacky!?" came back.

She ran home.

#6

#6

It was a funny kind of day - closed in. The sprinkler went lickety-split across the lawn catching at the sidewalk and painting the cement a truer, muddy brown. He dodged the spray and claimed the soggy log that was his local newspaper from the ivy bed that circled the birch. Manicured. His yard was manicured as were all the other yards lined up side by side like cemetery plots with houses for headstones. He shivered at the idea. Death was on his mind. He'd beaten the odds and then some. All he had to do was focus on his will - maintain the machine that was his body. It had served him well. He felt a muscle twinge in his throwing arm just above the wrist and rubbed it compensating for some lack of oxygen in the blood supply.

His house was white. The one diagonally across was grey - freshly painted by new neighbors he would never get to know - didn't care to. Twenty years of living lay in-between them and it didn't matter much that they were old - he was older. His patch was marked off neatly with whitewashed bricks shoved into the ground at an angle so that side by side, they seemed a low-down zigzag no one ever crossed. There might have been a sign - *Stay off the Grass* - there wasn't but there might have been. No crab grass, no weed, no dandelion, nobody ever trespassed on the old man's lawn so he summoned his indignation and relived last Tuesday or was it Monday when that collie dog had shat on the strip that ran between the sidewalk and the street.

You mind?!" he muttered recalling his stance on the porch - a thigh muscle twitched near his groin.

The owner of the dog had looked up taking in the source. The old man had squared his shoulders and narrowed one eye to a pitcher's slit. It was no use feigning innocence. The dog owner was younger - one of the new old boys - but clearly out of line. So what if the old man's body sagged on his skeleton like some other player's uniform two sizes too big. He held his stance and watched the other guy pull balled-up Kleenex from his pocket and lift the shit and wedge it down the gutter.

The old man had voted for the leash laws and would have voted for *No Dogs Allowed* had it been brought to the floor. He had voted for *No Soliciting* and *No Washlines on Sunday* too. He'd also agreed to *No People Under 55* and *No Kids Except Grandkids on Assorted Holidays and Weekends*. His wife kept telling him to put his hand down. *No Parking on the Street* had annoyed him and he'd kept his hand down for that but since the vote went against him, he found it a relief to see his community more park than parking lot. The list of nos went on. By-laws for the old. Nothing marred this quiet. This generation of his - depression era runts - cut off at their dreams - each still living for the next dime - they enforced this quiet. They demanded it. They'd been short-changed. Their youths hung shadows on their lives. Anzio crackled in his head clearer than what he had for breakfast. The Great War was his Father's war. Born to war. He'd lost his only son in Viet Nam. His sister divorced her husband when he came back off his head from Korea. They called it the Korean Conflict - those bigwigs down in Washington. Conflict - *balls* - as if renaming war would somehow wipe the slate. Politicians - crooks. The old man spat. They'd been through too much - this generation of his - not surprising then that in the end they'd come together for one last rank and file. G. I. loans had more or less paid for every plot. This community of theirs was zoned for peace.

The mourning dove cooed. The old man looked up to the roof. The bird stood still on the peak - a grey cutout. The coo lingered. Swallowed - forsaken sound. It thrilled the old man. Death's tole from a rooftop. He took a step back into the dark that was gathering on his porch and listened to the coo. He needed to be anonymous -

just another old man. All his life he hid - just another ticket. When he went out to the stadium - rare now - he passed by the players' entrance. He knew where it was. Even after they gutted the house that Ruth built and replaced it with Steinbrenner's stadium, he found it. Standing in the dun, he'd watch the entrance and remember the boy who stood outside waiting for Gehrig. He'd recall the way that Gehrig moved. He was there when Gehrig said good-bye to baseball. For a long time, there'd only been a few retired numbers out beyond center field. It was a rare place - set aside for the likes of number 4, number 3, number 7... The old man had seen them all play. Then Steinbrenner bought the Yankees and played god with the players' records. Who'd Steinbrenner think he was? Steinbrenner was an *asshole* - that's who. He made that place in center field commonplace. No number hung in center field for the old man - *should have been.* He didn't care. He was tired of stinkin' disappointment and never getting' there and never makin' ends meet. He was glad his wife was dead. He was glad not to have her worries in his head. He was glad to be just another fan. That's all he was. That's all he ever amounted to.

The yellow in the streetlight came on and backlit a boy. He was standing on the old man's lawn. He was kicking up a tuft of grass. He had spikes on.

"Hey-y-" The old man stepped out of the dark.

The boy didn't move.

"Get off the lawn!"

The boy did. He dropped off the curb, and crossed under the streetlight to the other side of the street. He stepped up on the neighbor's lawn and walked off to the distance. The old man watched him go. He was an awkward boy - beefy for his age. He had knickers on like he'd just come off a game. There weren't supposed to be any kids around here.

Kids aren't allowed.

The sun slipped off the horizon like a home run hit by Mantle, Mays, or Ruth. Distant pines tipped in pink stood watch like the outfield fence. The boy was gone off in the dark. The old man perused the street. It looked like nobody was home. Everybody had TV rooms on the backs of their houses and nobody in his generation wasted electricity. The whole neighborhood was dark except for the streetlight at the edge of the old man's property and the one at the corner.

He missed his wife. At night he missed her more. He'd watch her snooze - a gentle sputter in her lips until she snored herself awake. Then she'd smile apologetically for the snore he supposed or for leaving him to watch TV alone. In those final months, she hadn't been herself. That spark that was the girl's he'd married didn't lift her face. She was tired - said so. She kept saying he'd be the first to go but all along, the old man knew better. Death was as impossible to him now as it had been when he played ball - pickup games - back lots. He felt cheated. There was no one left who remembered who he was. His wife was the last person alive to have seen him hit a line drive out past first.

Where'd ya' go?

He looked for her murmurs and small talk in the pool of light shimmering on their bedroom ceiling. They'd watch it together sometimes in the night. He liked the way the streetlight did that. It reminded him of Brooklyn. As a boy, there'd been a red electric sign outside his window. It was eight feet tall. Its shadow flashed silently across his ceiling every 30 seconds letter by red letter starting with the T at the top. Then the O, then the N, then the Y then the apostrophe S. The Evangelistas paid his Dad $11 a month for the air space outside his son's bedroom window.

Stee-ee-rike two!

It sounded in his dream and he felt himself thrown back to the bottom of the ninth - 2 outs - the tying run on first. He shifted hips and rocked his spikes into dirt. He sensed more than saw the catcher's signal then the windup and the ball was careening towards him and the swing and in that split time, sure knowledge that yes - he would connect - and bat and ball collided and his pals were on their feet yelling him onto 1st and in the slowed-down yardage, he met his challenge and pumped his thighs and touched base in sweet time and turned to see the other runner rounding 3rd - and then the throw! The dirt balled up like furor around the plate and hid the outcome. Then the umpire - Pinky O'Day from 10th Street - straightened like a hawk -

See-ee-afe!

The old man woke up to a slapping breeze and cleared his throat and listened. The blinds were up. The streetlight was outside. The old man let his chest rise and fall. He felt his breaths in his nostrils.

Still alive.

Then his wife was young and sturdy - her thighs were brown and muscular. He watched them spread and lift for him and then she was on a beach running, laughing - he tried to close the gap. He couldn't see himself but he knew he was there. The mourning dove cooed. It was on the roof. He waited for it to coo again. Then he was in Prospect Park and his Grandfather's walking stick was scattering pigeons like feed. It was his idea living here in this community. She said no. She said she didn't want to leave home. He could see her crying when the ornament from their wedding cake didn't show up in all the unpacking. *Home* - he never felt like he was home - except maybe in some sandlot in Brooklyn with his Mother calling him over the fence for supper. Ever since he went to work and then later when he started commuting from the suburbs, he never felt like he was home. Then all the men in the neighborhood where they'd raised their son started calling him *sir* or *the old guy down the street*. If he'd stayed there, Death would have found him for sure. It would have rolled down the street like United Parcel. It would have found the light on their front porch. His wife insisted on leaving it lit even after their boy was gone. Death would have reached in their windows. She always left them open even in the winter. Death would have found him and found him. The old man in his waking place sobbed. He wanted her.

Oh damn.

The old man let his skull sink back into the pillow. Long night. Sweat. The tying run had been his. He batted it in - it was his. He was the one put hope back in the dugout for that extra inning. That's all they got. They lost it in the bottom of the tenth. It was his final high school game. His last time at serious bat. And he didn't even know it. Nothing feels like the last time at seventeen. He'd gone back to sandlot ball for a while in his 20's. It was fun. He outclassed his pals but so what. He liked the horseplay and the nonsense. There was talk of a semi-pro league - he was out of work - but then the war came and that was that.

A quart of milk had turned the refrigerator sour. He pulled it out and smelled it then watched with interest as it slid into the drain. The white substance almost seemed alive. He dusted the furniture after she left but then he ran out of polish. She used to keep a can of Pledge under the sink and 2 more in the utility closet. He kept thinking she'd show up. He kept thinking she'd walk through the door. There'd she be. But when the last can only shot out air, he knew she wasn't coming. Her figurines and vases didn't twinkle anymore. The stuff she lugged around with them their whole lives had a thin veneer of dust. He'd read somewhere that 90% of all dust was human skin scales so he supposed it was him sticking to her things. Ironic. The insides of the house looked like somebody had closed it up and gone off. Well, she had - hadn't she? She'd gone off. She'd given up the ghost.

The outside was different. The grounds were his - his grass, his shrubs, his trees. He pruned 'em, he seeded 'em - they were his. There was a fresh paint job on the house. Some kids from over a way came by last summer. He hired them and watched them do it. The back of their shoulders gleamed with sweat and gold beating down from the sun. The last time the old man painted a house himself was with his son.

A good time.

The very order of the place hid the old man's years. It ate a decade. It'd fool anybody riding by in an automobile. The old man stooped and a pain slid up his left side. He straightened then he tried again. There was something in the grass. His fingers caught at it, then before he had to straighten up again, he got it. It was a hard ball with a tear in the seam. He turned it over in his palm. *Property - Twin Valley Colts* is what it said. How about that.

Over here, Pop!

The old man thought he heard it. He looked out across the lawns.

Over here, Daddy!

And he'd hit another fungo out to center field and watch his son scramble for position. His boy had been a competitor even then - even at 9. It was in him - the way he moved - the way he held his body. Like Pee Wee Reese. The Twin Valley Colts had finished up the 1952 Little League season with a 12-2 record and the pennant for the township.

"Need a hand?"

"Hey?!" The old man felt yanked - his heart thumped.

He turned and looked at the boy from last night - the one by the streetlight - he was 10 yards away on the lawn.

"I was in the neighborhood." The boy was coming at him; as he did, he punched his glove with his fist.

The old man threw the hard ball as hard as he could and the boy stepped back and pulled it out of the air. Then the boy let go a slider and the old man watched it coming - plenty of time - he reached and the ball came home but his fingers - *damn them* - wouldn't close in time and the ball fell on the grass like baby's dribble.

"What's in here?"

The boy slid under the hood of the automatic garage door and caught sight of the old man's mitt. He pulled it out and stroked the leather. For no good reason, the old man felt a thrill. The boy put the mitt carefully back in place. It nested in a chicken wire contraption the old man had rigged. Nothing was out of place in the old man's garage.

"Need a hand?"

"No."

The old man pushed the power mower out of the garage. The boy followed him as far as the porch. The old man pulled the cord and the lawnmower bucked and died. The boy shifted his weight to the right. The old man pulled the cord again and the lawnmower hummed to life. The boy turned on his left foot letting his right tap him into position. The old man revved the starter and took control of the mower. The boy released the hard ball into the crevice of the porch step and his glove shot out and caught the rebound. The old man hunched his shoulders into the power of the mower and followed it out across the grass. The boy released the hard ball into the crevice of the porch step and his glove shot out and caught the rebound.

And so it played - the old man and the lawnmower - the boy and the hard ball. The lawnmower hummed. The hard ball thumped each time it hit the cement. The morning grew into a bright, clear day. It sparkled in the yard shining a glare each time the old man turned and ran the mower due east. At intervals, when the old man stopped and rested shirtless, breathless, wet and hot, he'd hear the hard ball thump and thump and thump. The truth was the old man was feeling good.

Good enough to mow the back?

The old man thought he could but nobody around here mowed the front and the back in one day. Better not push his luck. Better not draw attention. The grass was so green. Later, he'd clip the edge with a special tool he had. The old man stopped. He'd finished in no time flat. He felt himself smile as he waited for the thump of the hard ball. It didn't come. The old man turned. The boy was gone.

The old man felt disappointed. He wanted somebody to see the job he'd done. He wanted somebody to know he could do it.

I can still do it.

The truth was his son had been the ballplayer. The truth was the old man had never seen a season like his son's. At 15, before his prime, the old man had taken a job as a delivery boy for a butcher at the meat market because it was the only job he could get, and then later, much later, spent his weeknights in the stands feeling his genes swept along the channel of glory by his son, and no, it wasn't the same but it was like it. They'd scouted his son. In high school, the scouts had come out and in that final game, his son came up with the goods - 2 RBI's and a home run in the bottom of the 9th.

How's that, Homer...

His wife called him Homer back then - never his given name - she called him Homer. And then that Thursday night, they were in the Ford driving back and he snapped.

Don't call me that!

And she never did. His son was dead.

The old man felt defeated - like a punching bag gone flat. He stood there on his lawn and looked at the diagonal paths of mowed-down grass. If he had the heart, he'd mow every other row back the other way - due west - and lay down a field of diamonds like they did at Yankee Stadium.

If he had the heart.

The old man awoke alert sputtering on his own spit, saliva viscous in his mouth. He tried to lift his head then let it go and looked at the crack in the ceiling. Shadow and light played along it.

Where am I?

He breathed letting his breath out in audible puffs. His heart was beating like a tom-tom. *Why?* Someone was in the room - unmistakably there. He could feel it.

"Who's there?"

His voice when he heard it lacked conviction. It sounded scared.

"Who's there?"

He'd slept the afternoon away. His body ached - every muscle - his tendons wary of more effort. He sat up on the edge of the bed in his sweat in his work clothes and knew he didn't have the heart for a shower. Besides he was hungry. That was a good sign. For the first time in a long time, he was hungry.

After a boiled hot dog on a ballpark bun with onions and mustard and sweet relish, he went out back to check for ripe tomatoes. There were two. He picked one and ate it letting the juices leak down his neck and mingle with his sweat. Then he went to check her gardens. The zinnias stood up straight and yellow; the begonias sat in pink and white huddles. His wife had planted them herself earlier in the Spring. There were violets close to the foundation and some mountain purple. Those two re-seeded themselves and would be here for a long time. Her roses were at the far end where they'd get the most sun. They were deep and red and full. Beyond the roses - in the street, the boy stood looking up glove extended palm-up waiting for the ball.

He wore a cap this time as well as knickers. He took a step back and shuffled. The hardball landed in his glove. Except there was no sound. No sock of ball hitting leather. The old man pulled his ear. Dusk erased the youth's vitality and made him seem a tintype in the gathering night. The boy reached back and threw the ball straight up. Still no sound. No grunt. No effort. The old man took a step closer and as he did, the streetlight above the boy snapped to life.

"Boy?"

"Yessir. I'm here."

And the old man struggled with his joints across the lawn. He needed to walk more - *hell* - he needed to walk - *period*. Then he could mow the front and the back in one day and not feel like an old man. It would only take a minute more to cross the lawn. He hoped the boy would wait. And then when he got there - to the sidewalk - the boy was looking up into the yellow cone of streetlight. So the old man looked up too. It was as good excuse as any to catch his breath. There were gnats snarled up in the light.

"You play around here?"

The boy smiled not much. "There's always a lot. Somethin'. Play a pickup game. You know."

The old man concentrated on each breath pulling it in, letting it out. And he watched the gnats.

"Uh-huh. Around here?"

"A few streets over."

They were still looking up. The ball had not returned. *Or had it?* The old man watched the boy pull off his glove and tuck it in under his arm.

"You got a team?" The old man started looking for the ball along the curb.

"Yessir." The boy was closer. He had a sort of look on his face. He looked like a boy nobody wanted.

"Sandlot ball - that your game?" The old man looked down his nose - easier to focus.

The boy didn't like the scrutiny. He stepped back. He was bigger - not just taller - bigger than the old man had thought. He could probably really whack a ball.

"I'm a sandlotter myself. Started there. Brooklyn, New York - fourth largest city in the world." Confident, the old man sucked in air through his nose.

"Yessir." The boy watched him.

And the old man talked about himself - about school days and hot dog vendors and Yankee Stadium and his Dad - about Prospect Park and summer nights and curve balls and batting lefty - about stray dogs and fire escapes and horseshit in the streets - about fire engines and whistles and bells clanging in the night.

"That's why we moved to Jersey. Too much racket. When I was young, there was too much racket!" The old man said it like an accusation but he didn't mean it like that.

And then he and the boy talked about the greats - about Ruth, and Gehrig and PeeWee Reese - about Mantle and Mays and Berra - about Reggie Jackson and George Brett - about Ted Williams...

"Benny Bengough." The boy said the name.

"What about him?"

"You were a catcher, right? Sir?"

"That's my position."

"You ever seen Benny play, sir?"

It took the old man a minute. "Little guy."

"Yeah. But he knew what he was doin'." The boy sounded defensive. "He knew the game."

"How'd you know about Benny Bengough?"

"Oh, I know the game. I been knowing it since I was six."

"Six?" said the old man.

"Yessir. I know a lot."

The old man couldn't quite place Benny Bengough in the lineup, but he remembered the name all right. The kid was a real aficionado. They kept on talking - about how the game had changed - about the pitcher's mound - about spitballs - about Wrigley Field - about Pete Rose and how he shamed the game. The kid got uncomfortable talking about Rose so the old man switched gears.

"We gotta' get Billy Martin outa' Center Field." The old man believed this strongly. "His number doesn't belong out there with Ruth and Mantle."

"You should let him stay. Sir."

The old man felt surprised.

"He coulda' been one of the greats." The boy said it with a kind of affection and he said it with certainty.

The old man regarded him. It was dark all around them standing in the streetlight. The boy was old beyond his years.

"It's time to go." The boy was already on his way out of the light.

The old man felt disappointment. It had been years since he talked baseball.

"You have to go?"

"It's time, sir."

The old man noticed *Saint Mary's* sewn in neat block letters across the back of the boy's shirt and he watched it go until it was gone in the dark. The sound of crickets chirruping was all of a sudden loud to him. And then the old man heard the pop of a ball hitting pavement - then the bounce - then another bounce and the old man looked to see but he couldn't in the dark. Then the hard ball rolled in along the curb into the yellow air under the streetlight and stopped in the grate on the gutter at the old man's feet.

"Just a trick. Sir!" The kid's voice came out of the dark. The old man couldn't see him. "Some of us fellows play. You ain't scared?"

"Nope!"

"Some guys are yella'. They run home in the dark cryin' for their Ma."

"I'm not yella'!"

The truth was the old man was plenty scared - a ball coming out of dark like that. Of course the kid probably threw it up into the air after he got off aways. *Yeah, that was it.*

"I'd like to know that trick!" he called out.

Nothing came back. The old man thought the kid was gone. But then from a real distance, he heard the kid say "Next time."

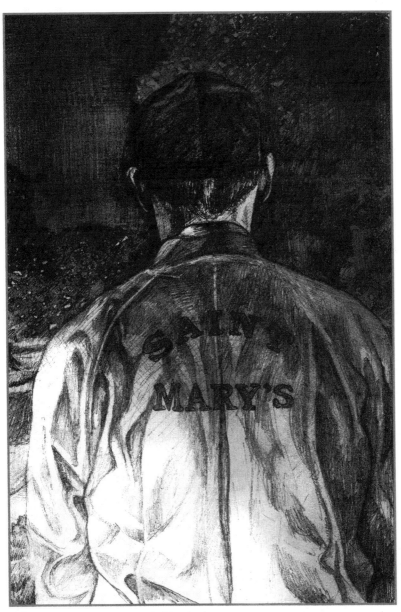

Nothing feels like the last time at seventeen.

The next day was his. It was Saturday. The old man felt invigorated - alive. It wasn't just the baseball talk - it wasn't just their mutual love of the game - it was the Yankees vs. the Mets. They were taking each other on that very afternoon - exhibition game. And *okay* it wasn't the old Dodgers but it was the Yankees on the tube on a Saturday afternoon with somebody to kibitz with about the game.

He drove to the supermarket and battled shopping carts to get a quart bottle of Bud, and a liter of Coke for the boy. He splurged on Wise potato chips and Quinlan pretzels, two personal favorites, and picked up a pack of Ballpark Franks in case they got hungry. He figured every kid in America liked a hot dog.

On his way home, he damn near hit a dog. That bothered him. He'd swerved in time but he needed to be more careful. He was glad though not to have to spend all day in some veterinarian's office or the police station instead of with the boy. But then the boy didn't come. It got to be 2:00 PM. Time for the game! The old man looked out his screen door. But the boy didn't come. The first pitch - *stree-ike one!* But the boy didn't come. The old man shuffled between the den and the front window. He looked out through the picture glass and hoped. But the boy didn't come. It got to be the bottom of the 3rd when he thought he heard somebody in the garage. He got up and looked but nobody was there. The old man gave up hoping at the 7th inning stretch.

Take me out to the ballgame - take me out with the crowd...

The old man heard the words in his head. They were playing his tune. But he sat in his easy chair and sagged under the disappointment. It wasn't a good game: Yankees 2 – Mets 1. No fun. What'd he expect? The kid was a kid. It was no use depending on him. The game would have been better too at the ballpark; the slow ones always were. The old man hadn't been back to see the insides of Yankee Stadium in years.

Buy me some peanuts and crack-er jacks...

The old man got an idea. He got up and went to the phone and called Yankee Stadium and charged 2 seats behind 3rd base for the following day. It was a double header. And *okay* they weren't the best seats in the house but the game held a kind of magic at the ballpark. The tube couldn't compete. Sparkling green magic - that and flat beer - no matter what at the ballpark. And the boy would come. The boy had to come.

The next day, the old man got in the car with his hands on the wheel and waited looking in the rear view and side view mirrors every 5 seconds hoping. He didn't know what he'd do if the boy didn't come. He didn't know if he'd go to the game at all. He didn't know what he'd do.

But then the car door on the passenger side popped open and the boy slid onto the front seat. He had on a blue jacket - the kind pitchers wear to keep their arm warmed-up. The cuffs were full of threads; one of the elbows was worn out. The kid was a real mess.

"Where's the ball? Sir. You got the ball?"

"Glove compartment. Buckle up."

The kid popped the glove compartment, pulled out the hardball, opened his glove and placed it gently in the sweet spot.

"It's there if you want it. Sir. All you have to do is reach out and grab it. It's yours." the boy said.

The old man backed out of the drive. He didn't like doubletalk - made him feel funny.

"Your seat belt. Put it on." And he indicated his by pulling at the strap.

For a while, the boy struggled with the tension on the seat belt while the old man drove.

"Not that way. Not like that. There's nuthin' wrong with that seat belt. Stop that! No. Buckle it!"

The truth was the old man was upset with the boy for being late and for not coming to the Saturday game and the boy was a lot bigger than he'd thought too - not too big for a seat belt - but big enough to be uncomfortable within the confines of the American made compact car the old man drove. At the stop for the toll booth, the old man buckled the seat belt for the boy.

The boy was interested in everything he saw. He didn't talk much but along the way up the Jersey Turnpike near the Newark Airport, the boy kept holding his ears and turning his head this way and that trying to see. Then he'd get trapped in his seatbelt - all twisted up.

"Sit still."

But the boy couldn't.

And there was something else too. He wasn't a boy. A kid, sure - to the old man - a kid. But to some, he would stand as a man now that the old man could take a good look. And he shouldn't have been squirming like that in his seatbelt.

When they got to the parking lot at Yankee Stadium which took some real doing since the old man hadn't driven in the city for a while, the old man took a moment to regain his senses. The traffic was unimaginable. Once they hit the bridge, everyone started honking and riding tailgate including the old man who'd had just about enough after the fifth cab cut him off and the woman in the backseat gave him the finger.

The boy was shocked. "Did you see that? Sir. Did you see that? A lady giving the finger…imagine that."

They got stuck in the gridlock on the Cross-Bronx Expressway and would have stayed stuck if the boy hadn't buffaloed a traffic cop by telling him "I gotta' make the game, officer - can ya' help us out?"

And the cop for reasons of his own motioned them across two lanes of angry cars onto the shoulder and directed them up the exit ramp with directions on the backway to the stadium.

Good to know.

There was something about the boy - no question. Pudgy face aside, there was a gleam to him like the finish on a new car when the sunlight hits it or the way a baseball diamond shines at a night game. With the kid, it came from inside and gleamed in his eyes like soft leather.

"1927."

"23. Sir."

"1927. Look at the averages."

"That's just it. Sir."

"He had a .362 batting average that year," objected the old man.

".393 in '23," countered the boy.

"60 home runs,' said the old man.

"That ain't the whole story. Sir. Look at the slugging average in the series."

"800."

"1000 in '23. Sir."

They were arguing Babe Ruth's best year, and the old man was scratching his mind for statistics. He wasn't sure of that last .800. It could have 1.000. *No, that was '28.* The boy was a record book of information although there'd been a time when the old man knew it all too.

Yankee Stadium didn't look all that different. Newer. More like it used to be when he was a boy before the gritty-grime of the Bronx had stained its façade. *Well, hell...*maybe he had to hand it to Steinbrenner. It was good seeing a facsimile of the old stadium from the outside. The hawk of vendors up and down the street, the rough and tumble of the crowd, the sound of the subway overhead, the smell of popcorn, the pennants on the breeze - they all brought back his Dad and his Grandpa and his son.

The ticket vendor waved the boy through the turnstile before the old man had a chance to give his name in for the reservations.

"Hold on! Can't ya' wait?!" The old man felt panic as the boy slipped into the cavern that arched up under the stands.

"This one's on us." The ticket vendor winked then waved the old man through.

Well, I'll be damned...

The old man struggled to catch up to the boy. It was probably old timer's day. He hadn't checked. Some kind of promotional deal - everybody over 75 in for free - *bring your Medicare card, guys* - somethin' like that. The boy was a good 20 yards ahead of him and going the wrong way, if memory served.

"You're goin' the wrong way!"

He didn't think the boy could hear him and if he did, he didn't care. The old man had a good mind to turn back but just then the boy took a left and disappeared from view. It took the old man a minute catching up. The pace the boy was setting left the old man sweating like a pig.

It was a tunnel. The old man shivered. It was low and dark. It was a low, dark tunnel that curved down into a deep pool of darkness. Way off - maybe 30 yards in, there was a yellow lightbulb coming out of the wall. It was lit up but not doing much to cut down on the darkness. No distant arch of sunlight promised the game though the old man knew if he followed the tunnel in, it had to eventually come out at the box seats - *had to.*

That's when the boy appeared in the yellow light thrown by the lightbulb. He walked right through it like he knew where he was going. And then, he was gone again.

"Hey-y! Boy! Wait up!"

And the old man plunged in. It occurred to him that he hadn't asked the boy his name. And the boy didn't know his name either. *Funny.* The kid's name would have come in handy - he could have yelled it out. There was water dripping somewhere. *Water dripping.* Like an echo. *A leaky tap. Janitor's closet.* The old man heard it go by him in the dark. He moved on towards the yellow lightbulb up ahead. He licked his lips - he felt funny. His shoes snapped on wooden slats underfoot. That was a nice touch - Steinbrenner again?

The old man felt grateful not to feel cement pressing up against the blood blisters on the back of his toes. He was tired of cement. Cement and cement - everywhere cement. Or worse - asphalt and potholes. Tripping you up - making your feet tired. They were covering up the world in black asphalt and cement. The old man remembered reading somewhere - in fast food restaurants, they made seats too small for the average behind so the average customer would hurry up and eat and move on - keep moving on. That's what asphalt and cement felt like to the old man - like moving on.

The old man got in the yellow light thrown by the lightbulb and stopped. It was funny being in the yellow light. He could just get his whole body in it. If he spread out his arms, they disappeared into pitch blackness. Both ways out from the old man were pitch black and the daylight from the arcade that ran under the stadium wasn't visible anymore. The tunnel must have curved around and cut it off. The old man thought about going back - about getting out of here. He couldn't see where he was going and he didn't like that.

"Yo." It came out of the tunnel up ahead. It was a soft call.

The old man stepped out of the yellow into the pitch black. He slid his shoes along the slats underfoot. His hearing felt sharper. Probably because of the dark. But he thought the voice had come from the right. Was there another way off to the right? The old man peered into the dark and saw a deeper shade. He slid his arm along and the wall opened up.

Inky fog wet the old man's brow. It was cooler in this tunnel. All he could see was blackness. No lights up ahead. All he could hear was the swish and whoosh of his own heartbeat pulsing inside his head. *Where's the boy?*

"Ah - the heck with it!" He said it out loud and he said it in disgust.

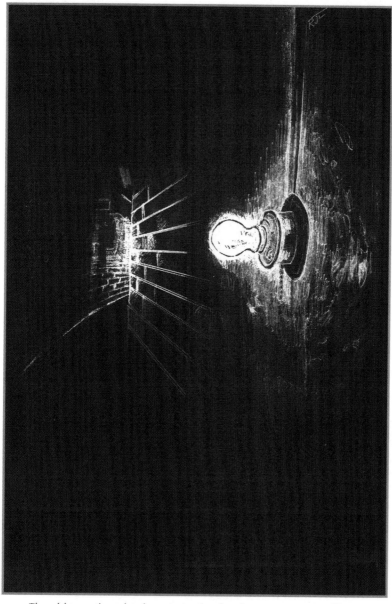

The old man thought about going back - about getting out of here.

The old man didn't have time to play games. He'd be damned if he was going to waste the day running around in the dark after some kid. He turned back. But then a draft brushed up against the nape of his neck. It caught him by surprise.

There's gotta' be a door - a way out.

And as he thought it, a tumbler rolled over in its lock. It sounded loud. As the old man turned around, a door swung open on a breath and lay down a path of yellow light.

"So it's me versus them and vice-a-versa." The Brooklyn accent sounded like home. "I mean - I started fearin' for my life."

Laughter. Guys laughing.

The old man stood there and listened.

"The two of d'em are out there runnin' a-round hollerin' for the ball, crackin' into each other's skulls like there' nobody rounding second and I yell out 'Get outa' the way, you meatballs - what is this? The prom?'"

More laughter. The old man felt a smile tugging at his lips.

"I told the management - that's it! I'm playing right field. I ain't standin' out there in the middle of center with them two clowns for backup!"

"Whadda' ya' mean - backup?!" It was a challenge coming from deeper inside the yellow light.

"Backup?!" Brooklyn's clear nasal shot back - "What backup?! I'm out there in the middle of Ringling Brothers Barnum Bailey Circus."

"Lemme' explain somethin' to you!"

"I'm all ears!"

"Without me-!" The emphasis was on *me*.

"Yeah-h?" Brooklyn dragged out the word like a slow call.

"Without me-"

"Yeah?!"

The old man held his breath - the laughter waited.

"With-out me!" The other voice was getting real deliberate. "You're out there in center or right or anywheres you wanna' and your spikes is full of cow manure!"

The old man and the laughter roared.

God.

It was fun - the sheer nonsense of it - the tomfoolery. The old man missed it - the ribbing - the love of the game. His stomach hurt from laugher.

"Hey - what're ya' doin' there?" It was Brooklyn.

He was standing like a shadow in the doorway backlit by the yellow light. The old man could make out a baseball cap. Brooklyn's stance looked familiar - sturdy, small, well-built.

"Hey, Jidge!" Brooklyn called back to somebody in the room. "There's a guy here for ya'." Then he wandered off into the light.

The old man took the distance to the door with determination. He wanted to see. He needed to see. He was sick of always being on the outs - never stepping up to the plate. Always hid. He was always hid. His whole life was from the stands of disappointment. The guys who knew he could play were gone with his boyhood. Even his son - his son never knew just how good his Dad really was. His stats were lost forever. Like some pipe dream. Like he made it up.

And how many times could you tell about this save or that play without somebody there backing you up? Givin' you the go ahead. Lettin' the people know who you were once in your whole stinkin' life.

When he stepped into the path of yellow light that ran down from the open doorway, he felt a draft lift the hair on his forearms and a chill run through his chest like a wave. But the lure of the game was too strong. The old man didn't hesitate - in he went.

50

The New York Yankee pinstripe was everywhere - open-shirted hanging ready on locker doors. Athletes moved deliberately through the room pulling at their socks, smoothing down their knickerbockers, lacing up their spikes. Somebody brushed his shoulder passing by and then the sweet smell of tangy sweat stung the old man's nostrils. The room was seasoned with it. And he couldn't quite believe he was here.

"Hey, pal. You ever hear of bein' punctual?" It was Billy Martin. "You're way overdue." And he poked his index finger into the old man's chest.

"Ah, lay offa' him." It was the boy.

The old man recognized the voice, but when he turned, the boy wasn't there. Then he felt himself being not so gently nudged through a maze of athletes to a string of lockers.

"You better suit up." It was Brooklyn behind him. "We got five minutes tops before they announce us for the game."

The old man found himself in front of locker #6. It was dark green metal and it had the number 6 in white painted on the door.

"Go 'awn. Open it up," urged Brooklyn.

"Am I dead?" The old man didn't want the answer.

Brooklyn lowered his voice. "Yeah. You could say d'at in one sense of the word. Keep it down, will ya'? There's a couple guys in here ain't caught on."

So he'd been had. Death had found him out, and the old man hadn't even seen it coming.

"The big guy's a master at d'is. No way you coulda' figured it." It was still Brooklyn. "Besides nuthin' lasts forever."

"Dead's dead," said the old man.

"Oh yeah?" challenged Brooklyn. "Tell me - how do ya' feel?"

The old man thought about it and the truth was he was feeling pretty good.

"See-ee." Brooklyn's face lit up like a beam.

The old man watched his own hand lift and release the locker door - no liver spots. There was a uniform hangered lop-sided inside and a sweaty cap. A pair of spikes were laced together and hanging off a hook. Dried mud was embedded in the spikes. It lined the sole of the shoes like icing.

"Sorry 'bout d'at" said Brooklyn. "Wally was in a hurry getting' outa' here."

The old man unbuttoned his sportshirt; it felt tight on him.

"D'at's the guy you're replacin' in the roster" Brooklyn went on; "Good hands - he got traded up."

The old man unbuttoned his pants and looked down at the hambones that were his thighs.

"The big guy says you're sumthin'. The big guy says you got it." Brooklyn was trying to make him feel good.

"Is Lou Gehrig here?" The old man felt foolish asking but he'd always wanted to meet number 4.

"Nah" said Brooklyn. "He was in and outa' here like a shot. Good attendance. Good everything. The guy was just plain good."

"All Yankees here" the old man realized.

"Yeah. An' those that shoulda' been."

The old man didn't want to ask Brooklyn his name. It would have been an insult. He was a player - no question. Not one of the all time greats but still a major leaguer. Probably going back some. The old man almost had it - shortstop - no third base.

Brooklyn was still talking."...yeah, we get a lotta' catchers in here. The big guy keeps hopin' Benny'll come through."

"Benny Bengough." said the old man.

"Yeah. You seen him?"

"No."

"They were pals - the big guy and Benny." Brooklyn was looking around.

The locker room was clearing out.

"Lissen, I gotta' get ready myself." Brooklyn pulled up off the bench. "This is your shot, fella'. Take it."

There was a guy in the corner - looked like Bob Meusel. *Hell,* it probably was Bob Meusel. The old man slipped the uniform off the hanger.

"Time!" somebody shouted out from somewhere and then a door banged shut.

The old man suited up. He'd waited for this moment all his life and now that it was here, he couldn't hold back. *No regrets.* Somebody would notice the backyard needed mowing - the newspapers piling up - the mail overstuffed in the box. Not that he'd gotten much mail of late. The truth was nobody there would give a damn he was gone.

"You ready?" It was the boy.

The old man turned to face him but he wasn't a boy anymore. *No, he wouldn't be.* He was a big ape of a guy with a tuft of dark hair and a squashed-in melon face.

"Babe?" said the old man.

"They call me Jidge. My friends - call me Jidge."

"Jidge" repeated the old man - he was almost afraid to say it.

"That's right" said Babe Ruth.

Self-conscious, the old man examined his cap and then he pulled it on.

Babe Ruth watched him do it.

Then the old man spotted his old catcher's mitt tucked in the corner of the locker shelf. He pulled it loose and stroked the leather.

"I got it outa' the garage." said Babe Ruth. "I figured you'd need it."

"Thanks." said the old man; he was glad to have it.

Babe Ruth tugged at the brim of his own cap and turned to go. The old man followed him out of the locker room. When he turned the corner, the old man looked up into a field of light. It sparkled and propelled itself down the runway like a star. The old man stepped back. Babe Ruth caught him on the shoulder. In the center of the light, a baseball hung and shimmered like a sun.

"Don't turn yella' - it's yours" said Babe Ruth.

The old man felt the reassurance surge through him like adrenaline.

"I'm sorry I didn't recognize you," he said.

"It don't matter. I recognized you, Homer."

And they walked up into the light together - number 3 and number 6.

Madame Toullaine and
the Big Red Head

Madame Toullaine and the Big Red Head

Toot

"Pleasure bunny - she's a pleasure bunny," Bill said. Then he squeaked saliva out his two front teeth.

Toot had a toothpick stuck in-between 2 molars that laid out his lips in a lopsided grin.

"Where?"

"There."

Toot looked hard at the rearend of the customer in aisle 3. It was bent over and wide and he considered it. Toot thought he agreed with Bill on this. At the top of the legs, there were two little indents in the middle where he could see through to a lemon tank top filled up with 2 very delicious looking *bazookas*. And besides the way she had her legs turned out just a little bit intensified the shape of her behind and was, Toot knew from fairly intense experience, the mating call of female shoppers to stock boys everywhere.

"Told ya'. Go 'awn. See if you can get her."

Toot pulled out the toothpick and grabbed hold of the ferry. There was thirty 12-paks of store-brand soda that needed a display. The rearend as he approached it straightened up dissolving down into 2 neatly shaped blue cheeks. He let his eyes follow on up the bare-backed halter to the creamy colored freckles on the shapely shoulders to the long slim neck to the golden bangle earrings. Her hair had the sunset in it. She had a short doo - a feather cut his

Mom would say. Toot sailed the ferry past her and did not look back.

With his excellent peripheral vision, he could see she was definitely not jail bait - *first base coming up*. Toot parked the ferry and walked back casual on a slow slide like he was looking for something that just might be in aisle 3 and *gotcha'* she watched him the whole time he was coming. Toot rolled his right shoulder up on a slow machination forward like it was oiled and worthy of individual attention which it was - then he down shifted his pelvis, dropped his chin and brought the left shoulder up on a nice clean push forward and then the roll and then the chin up and straight out and then the right shoulder up and so on. His forearms he let down into 2 fists muscles-tensed for size and definition all the while sending the message he knew she wanted to hear.

"What?" She grinned - blue terrific eyes.

"You look like - a pol-ka dot," he was grinning the way he knew she liked it.

"Yeah - so."

"Like a pol-ka dotted baby doll. I never seen the likes."

"Yeah - so?"

"I was jus' - nuthin' - that's all." *Lie* - all he could think about was her polka-dotted tummy and whether she had an inny or an outy for a belly button.

"Who you think y'are?" She had a box of Pop Tarts in her left hand - *no rings - check it out*.

Lynne Doddie

She was checking the price on a box of Pop Tarts. He was checking out her left hand so she flicked her ring finger against her thumb and made a sort of *tick* sound up and down the aisle. *Keep your mind off my freckles*. Lynne Doddie hated freckles and she was 25 years old. She pumped gas at the old works outside of town and mostly truckers came in and this kid made her want to laugh and cry. She knew him. She watched him grow up behind her. She slid the Pop Tarts back into their strawberry slot on the shelf. He was old enough now.

"So - what?"

He was losing his nerve. She could see it draining out of him. She started down the aisle with her cart so he had to hurry up and turn around and move his cart out of her way. She thought about giving him a break. It'd been a long night - the regular 7:00 AM guy didn't show up at his regular time. It was past 9:00 AM when he pulled in. She was squat on the cement stoop outside the office trying to hold it together. It was a good thing too because a line of E-Macks pulled in just then and if she'd had to go out there and service them, she would have dropped dead. Lynne Doddie hated the 7:00 AM guy. He was overly familiar. *Fresh.* And he took regular advantage of her by showing up late. That said - he was related to the owner of the works in some way so she knew she had to take it. She turned to the kid and told him it was Wednesday and her night off.

He stopped breathing. It was visible.

"So how about we hook up here and head out to the Blue Angel. How's that?"

She left him standing there in his own daze. She already had half-regret she let him in on her only night off. He watched her checking out - the whole time. When she stashed her groceries in the back seat and got in her car, his buddy was staring from behind the sheet glass that fronted the supermarket.

Back at her place, there was dirt in the screens on the sitting porch which pissed her off on account of the new curtains. She tapped at it with her fingernails. The screens needed a rinse. The ruffle on the new curtains held a perfect frill. She loved fluff - the way it made the light curl. She had a feather mattress cover from the home shopping channel that would make her feel like she was sinking into a dream after her morning steam in a bath of jasmine and jade *Olio*. *Olio* was a brand name she thought was dumb - it sounded like margarine. But she sure liked the flavor.

Her dog, Bouser, watched her lose the tension and the grime she got on the job. The pay was good - no complaints. She was pulling in 20 bucks an hour. But the night shift after about 2:00 AM was non-stop. She pumped gas and checked out pressure and oil and whatever the hell else came up. She was still young - in a way. The kid in the supermarket confirmed that. *Imagine* - a kid like that going after her. Well, he made her pay attention, didn't he? The water in the tub steamed and got in-between her legs and under her arms and was working on her spine. She had a little balloon pillow under her neck. The steam was taking her down and *oh God* it felt good.

When she dreamed, she dreamed about a highway and dirt and a line of haulers coming one after another down the pike their headlights smudged by a dust storm. They were coming at her non-stop and she couldn't stay clean on account of the storm. It was on every inch of her. It filled in the spaces between the freckles and her hair was powdered with dry mud. The storm was getting worse obliterating even the headlights now but the sounds of the engines came at her low and loud. They were droning at her like an army caravan. The wind had no mercy - it drove in waves as hauler after hauler whipped past on a rush. It caught in her breath and filled her nose with soot. She couldn't breathe. She tried to get up. Lynne Doddie tried to get up out of her dream, but she couldn't. Something was making her pay attention. Then there was this huge hauler pulled to a stop at the pumps a story- high out of nowhere and a big fat guy with butch red hair and freckles looking down out of the cab yelling something - *BAIT!* She heard it - *BAIT!* And it made her scream.

It was early night when she peeled up off her pillow in a sweat. She could see the blue fading in the blinds. It was dusk. Her elbows were dug down deep in the goose feathers. Her favorite pajamas were soaked. *What the hell.* BAIT! It kept running in her head like an alarm clock. BAIT! She could hear the haulers running underneath her bed. BAIT! And somebody screamed. She heard it. That's what woke her.

Lynne Doddie shot up off her bed. She walked around the room; she looked out in-between the blinds at the street. Nobody was out. Just her street. It was getting dark. An upstairs window came on at the corner. A pickup drove by - *no headlights.* Nobody was screaming.

She called Madame Toullaine with a cigarette in her mouth. She needed to talk. Toullaine was a pseudo-psychic like Whoopi Goldberg in the movie, *Ghost.* Sometimes she heard things - sometimes she saw things - sometimes she made it up. But that last she did only when she was trying to figure it. Toullaine would rattle around a problem until she made a hit - until something added up. Once Lynne Doddie saw her push back in her seat and flip over against the back wall. Toullaine was in her late 50's by all accounts at the time and even though she'd worked the trapeze as a kid, this move was a surprise even to Toullaine. They talked about it later over tea leaves; Toullaine really believed it was the spirit of her dead brother coming into her. She said her brother fell from the wire doing a flipover. She said when this happened, her Mother got mad at her Father and packed up Toullaine and herself and headed out of circus life forever.

"What a life." Lynne Doddie said it out loud out of admiration and respect.

The phone picked up. "Yeah?"

"Can we have something to eat?" Lynne Doddie really needed to talk.

"What time is it?"

When Madame Toullaine woke up - she worked the death watch on the drawbridge over on the bay - her voice sounded like the possessed kid's voice in *The Exorcist.*

"I can't think." Toullaine was struggling.

"It's Lynne. I need to talk."

"I know. I can hear it."

Toullaine

"BAIT - he just kept sayin' it." Lynne's voice had a trill in it. It was one of the things Toullaine liked about Lynne. The trill in her voice reminded her of her mother.

"Are ya' there?"

"Yeah. I'm thinkin'." Toullaine's throat hurt - it felt like somebody just *windexed* her chords. "You sure it was you he was talking to?"

"Nobody else was there." Lynne sounded petrified.

"I ain't so sure about this one. It could mean a lot of stuff."

"Gimme' a for instance," said Lynne from the other end.

"It could mean-n..." Toullaine picked up her clock off the nightstand. "You wanna' be a biker and just take off - ya' know?"

"A biker-"

"First thing struck me was the description. The red haircut. The freckles."

"So I wanna' go? Just get out of here?"

"This town's dead, Lynne. You know that. It's a shore town. You're young."

"Where would I go?"

"I don't know. Phillie?"

"Philadelphia?"

"It could mean-n...you're gonna' meet the right guy. Get married."

"I don't wanna' marry a fat butchy guy."

Toullaine pushed herself back into her pillows, spread her legs and flexed her toes. "It could mean this is your son grown up."

Jones

Lynne didn't have a son. "You know that."

"I mean on some future plane or possible future. It's all in the alternative. Look in the alternative. Count your alternatives. They're your wishes. This fat guy with the red hair was makin' you pay attention. What for?"

"I don't know." Lynne was calming down. Toullaine could hear it.

"The revving of the bikes!" It's was the most obvious thing. "It's loud, right?"

"Did I say he had a bike?"

That stopped Toullaine. She never questioned it. Maybe this was one of her insights.

"I don't know what you said, but the red head was a biker, trust me."

Lynne Doddie

Lynne was looking at the *Flamingo* on her nails. Time for a change.

"Is that it?" Toullaine's voice had dropped a register. It sounded mellower now like a fog horn.

"I guess. Maybe I can come over tonight?" She wasn't sure if going over there would jog something else out of Toullaine, not that that was the only reason for going over. Besides the dream was stupid. It was just a replay of her shift with a spooky dust storm thrown in.

"Bring some hoagies."

Food was the first and last thing on Toullaine's mind when she went through the change. She said she lost one thing but got another - *taste*. She made a joke - *First time in my life - I got - taste*. Lynne laughed at that one - the way she said it. But it was really true - everything tasted good to Toullaine when she went through the change. Except chocolate.

While she made her bed real smooth for the next time she got in, Lynne tried to think about *no sex*. Toullaine said she wasn't having it - *No more*. It must be tough but Toullaine was the most satisfied woman Lynne knew. Toullaine liked her life just the way it was which was more than Lynne Doddie could say. Sometimes Lynne thought about getting married. Doing the whole deal might be just the thing but *then what*? Two of her best friends got slugged on a semi-regular basis and the one - Jano - was with a real smooth guy too - Phil. Phil was good looking. He flirted with Lynne whenever she came over and always got her favorite, Rolling Rock beer, stocked in their fridge even though he himself preferred Miller. Jano would roll her eyes and later when the two of them were off doing some shopping say *The storm has passed - gimme' a break, God.*

Lynne was committed to not being like that. She didn't want to get trapped in a circle. She didn't want to do the same old thing over and over. Maybe it was that about the dream. The haulers kept coming not giving her a minute to breathe. Maybe it was that. Time to go - do something new. Toullaine kept telling her her aura was clean. That she was good. She didn't feel good. But Toullaine said she was and *why not*?

Toot

Toot didn't like the idea of being made to look like an *asshole*. He had a lot of shirts out. He was trying to look slick but not like he was trying to make an impression. *Assholes* like Ernie Carson made impressions on girls. *Gees*. Ernie was always talkin' about his clothes like he was a *fruit* or something. Toot had already narrowed it down to the shirt with the blue sheen his girlfriend gave him last birthday but the soft black one made his skin feel good. Toot tried to see in his mind how'd he look standing in the parking lot when she showed up. *Not cool* he decided. He could make the move like he just showed up. He could come walking out of the field that ran along the north end of the parking lot like he just got there - like it was a surprise she was waiting for him. *Oh, yeah - there y'are.* That way he could be there for her but not look it. There was a bunch of bayberry bushes in about 50 feet from the asphalt that gave him a view of the whole lot. He knew her car - a baby blue Chevrolet convertible - vintage. He liked that about her. A car said *here - take a look - this is me.* He knew her around town. She was captain of the cheerleaders when he was in 6th grade - a senior in high school. After the date they made in the cereal aisle, her placed her. *The Blue Angel - gees.*

Toot remembered Billy liked her that summer after 6th grade. He said he loved her. He said when he grew up, he was marrying her. He said it every day that whole summer vacation. Toot was looking in his mirror at himself a long time ago. Twelve was a good year for him. The trouble with the bushes was bugs. They were all over in there and he attracted them like flies. He wished he was like his Mother in this. His Mother never got bit. She could walk on the beach with a steady land breeze at dusk and never get bit.

"Ma, come in here." She had a good eye for some things.

"You come out here." She was watching the *The MacNeil/Lehrer Report.* She thought Robert MacNeil was nice looking and a decent man and she liked news - it was all she would watch. It was like she was waiting for something to be announced.

"I was wonderin' which one is good!" Toot didn't move from where he was standing in his room which was off the kitchen which was where she was.

"Have you got it narrowed down?" She was getting up from the table. The chair leg scraped the floor.

"The black one or the blue one?"

She was at the door to his room looking in at the shirts. "This is for Ginny?"

He felt like a dog all of a sudden.

"Not for Ginny then." His Mom could read him like a book. "Okay. What's she like?"

"She's - a - older woman."

"Ah, Toot."

"Nah. Not like that, Ma."

"You have to be good."

"Ma - I'm a-" He wanted to say *grown man* but it stuck in his throat. "She's a blond, Ma."

"A blond." His Mother was dark - true to her native heritage.

"Yeah."

She was looking at the shirts on his bed like she was getting vibes off them.

"The blue one," his Mother said and turned around in the doorway and headed back to the news.

Lynne Doddie

Lynne rode over there in a fog. There was one coming in off the ocean. She could hear the surf. The line on the road was like a ribbon of clean white leading her in and out of curves with her tires sucking up whispers off the blacktop. The fog wasn't settled yet - it was moving like smoke through the thin air just above the surface of the road.

Toullaine lived far out towards the north end of the peninsula - not really far out like Jerry - but far out. She had a single-story house up on pilings that came off the road like the one Joan Crawford had in *Mildred Pierce* but not swank. Lynne liked the drive out there with the salt air whipping in at the windows. She had the roof up. It was sand-colored canvas - the perfect addition to her baby blue car. It was going to rain. She could feel it. Lynne liked the rain and being alive and she realized living where she was by the sea. She didn't like her life though. There was something off.

There was a light up ahead far off in the dunes. The road went through the dunes almost on a straightaway but the effect was in and out because of the low hills and brush. Lynne liked to pick blueberries out here in late summer and then they'd go back to Toullaine's and make a pie - sometimes jelly. Lynne liked doing stuff like that but sometimes the loneliness really got her. It never got Toullaine. Toullaine fit right in. Lynne didn't fit - she never fit in. Everyday she felt like a stranger moving through the dark. *Why is that?* Her Mother used to say they almost didn't live here but then they did. She said they almost lived in Arizona. Lynne wondered about that. Would she fit in in Arizona? Arizona had sand and sunsets.

The light in the dunes was gone for a second then it came back on again moving like a moon of yellow coming through a cloudbank. Lynne thought back to a UFO she saw once off the deck of Toullaine's house. Toullaine saw it too. It whipped across the horizon just above sea level like a shot and all the lights up and down the beach went out. It was weird waiting all night in the pitch black for the lights to come back on. Toullaine has some old red lanterns they put up on the deck. Some people had flashlights out on the beach. They were calling to each other. Toullaine's next door neighbors made their way over - summer people. Then they all watched the dark together. Whatever the thing was, it didn't come back. The next day they heard on the news that there was a power outage due to insufficient amperage caused by the overuse of electrical wattage due to the heatwave. *Pish-sh-sh* was what Toullaine said. There was no heat wave. There was no overuse. Practically nobody on the shoreline owned an air conditioner let alone used it. It wasn't the city. Who needed an air conditioner with the ocean right here *blowing you in the face?* Then they said that the local sheriff's office had received several calls regarding a light in the sky but it turned out to be the McDonald's blimp. The two of them laughed at that one. Toullaine said *Yeah, sure, a blimp - traveling at the speed of light. Call Carl Sagan.*

The light was showing itself at regular intervals now. Not somebody fishing - that kind of light would waver but hold to its own spot. This light was getting closer. *Funny.* Nobody lived out there but Jerry. The state had a hold on building any new houses on the peninsula, until the legislature voted on the ocean park *for all the people* from Newark and all the cities that lined up the Hudson. *What a riot - politicians.* What were they gonna' do - bus a bunch of inner city families all the way down here and make them camp out? *Then what - mosquito bites all over?* Lynne Doddie thought about how come she got to live here and not some black kid from some project? There were blacks inland and down by Atlantic City but not here. Maybe she was lucky - living here. Maybe she should just settle down and thank God. The light blinked out but the low hum of a bike came at her through her rolled down window. Jerry the Fisherman drove a jeep. But this was a bike. Lynne felt funny all of a sudden. Like last night in the dream. Toullaine's wasn't that far off now; Lynne could just make out the post light. It was high up and blue. Without it, nobody'd know Toullaine's was there. They'd drive right past. BAIT! The water did funny things to sound but she heard it. BAIT! The hum of the bike was coming closer. *The red head was a biker, trust me -* Toullaine's words came back to her exactly. Lynne got scared. She didn't want to meet up with a nightmare. She pressed her foot down on the accelerator and headed out into the dunes. She'd get to Toullaine's before the bike got to her. And then she'd be safe. With Toullaine.

Toullaine

Toullaine was on the screened-in part of her porch with her bad foot up munching a peanut butter and jelly when Lynne's car slid out of the fog on a sudden hush and then disappeared. Toullaine stood up. She crossed to the screen door then out onto the 10 foot bridge that connected her to the road. Her post light was on. She looked up. Electric blue. She went out and stood in the middle of the road. The fog closed in around her fingering the folds of her robe. Toullaine looked as far down as she could. Red taillights faint and distant. *What's go-ing on?* There was nothing out there but Jerry. Maybe she should call Jerry. He had a phone. Sometimes he brought blue fish in and she cooked it. They ate it together on the porch. That was about as close as Jerry got to town. He had his own gas pump. Canned goods and dried goods stocked every 3 months. Jerry had an air raid shelter too. He lived his life in suspicion. *It's comin'* he said *It's comin' - believe me - it's comin'.* He never said what was comin' - just that it was and he was prepared. The only other people out there were his customers - fishermen that returned every summer. They stayed in his cabins. If the state came and made Jerry move out of there, it'd kill him. The distant sputter of a Harley came to her ears. *How far off?* It could be miles. It could be inland. Well, tonight, Jerry was getting a visit from Lynne Doddie and that was okay. Jerry like Lynne. Toullaine noticed the flag on her mailbox was up. She poked her hand inside - a flyer for the auction at the church. Then she crossed back to her house and went inside. Toullaine was a truster of fate.

Toot

Toot was alone in the bayberry bushes trying not to get messed up. There was a nip in the air tonight; it smelled like Fall. He had on his pressed leather jacket and it was too hot for it even with the chill but he didn't want to screw up the look so he left it on. He had admitted to himself standing in the bushes alone *This is important.* He wanted her. She was his type or at least the type he thought he deserved. He liked them blond with soft round bazooms ripe as tomatoes in a Jersey garden waiting for some lucky guy to pick. And he thought about her freckles all over them and how maybe her tit would feel in his mouth and he felt himself getting *a boner* so he shifted his attention to the parking lot. The lights in the parking lot were motion lights which was stupid but the summer crowd said the parking lot was an eyesore that didn't deserve getting lit up at night. This time of year with no traffic on the road, the motion lights stayed unlit and Toot had to stand there with nothing even to look at. He used to skateboard here on the asphalt with Billy. They'd come out summer nights; they'd set it all up with soda cans and make a ramp out of wood coming off the dumpster. And it was cool because when they came down off the ramp and made their moves through the cans, the motion lights would follow them and light up the dark in waves. Toot tried to remember the last time *him* and Billy did that. Something fading in his mind didn't like the idea that he'd never do that again. It had to be 8th grade - that summer he met Ginny. She was one of the summer people. She lived out on the lagoon from June 15th until Labor Day. Her Father had money. In July, Toot laid a roof on the extension B&B Construction built on her house and Ginny was always hanging around with her girlfriends swimming in the lagoon. She was a little pipsqueak of a thing with green eyes and long lashes. She used to show up at her bedroom window and talk to him while he laid the shingles. This summer that just passed, Ginny didn't come. There was a *For Sale* sign on her front lawn. *Shit.* A mosquito got him good on the back of the neck. He slapped at it and got the satisfaction of hearing its final *zizz* but when he pulled his palm away, he had blood on it and he knew he didn't have a Kleenex. Toot shrugged off his jacket and unbuttoned his blue shirt, the one that Ginny got, with his left hand but when he got it off, there was blood sinking into the crease in the collar. *Shit oh shit.* Toot wanted out of this town. He'd even gone up to the recruiting station in Asbury Park and checked out what the Marines had to say. They kept calling him up on the phone. Some Lieutenant. It made him feel like a man - somebody wanting him - like maybe he was somebody too - not just Ginny and her family. Toot felt bad when he thought of his Mom out at the beach all by herself but they'd always been alone so he figured she'd make it alright. Besides she was always saying *What am I waiting for?* Toot didn't want to be saying that at her age. But something was holding onto him. He felt it in his throat like the scratch that came just before a cold. Sometimes it was in the middle of his chest like a fist or something holding him back. He asked Billy about it once when they were having a couple of beers. The delivery door was up and the cattails were crackling in a pretty stiff breeze. Bill smoked reefer. Toot was saying how he couldn't stand it - thinking of his whole life here and Bill let go of some smoke and said, "It's nice here." Toot asked Bill if he ever felt like he was being held back by some thing. And Bill just shook his head and said *Whadda' ya' mean?* This bothered Toot. He always thought *him* and Bill would be pals his whole life. But now he could see - they were different.

Toot couldn't be still. His mind got filled up with so many ideas. Sometimes he felt like he'd explode. The only thing that calmed him down really was sex. He had a car he worked on - an old Plymouth. It taught him a lot - that car - and he'd catch his Mom watching him from inside the kitchen window. *What? Whadda' you want, Ma? What?* And he'd put down his wrench or whatever on the fender - ready to talk. But she'd just smile; she loved him. Toot wanted so much. But he didn't know how to get it. He didn't know how. And *shit* he didn't even know what it was he wanted - except getting out of here. Toot knew that.

Toullaine

Toullaine felt fog hit the glass sliders on her oceanside deck like a dull thud. It didn't make a sound. It was like a cat pouncing. It cut off everything between here and there for the mouse without making a sound. Sometimes the call of a ship came out of it or the ding-ding of a buoy but mostly fog was quiet. There was no going after Lynne. It'd been fifteen minutes. Toullaine didn't know how she missed the house. The light was lit. It was an old electric blue railroad light. It pierced the fog. Toullaine got a good feeling off it. Barney put up that light. So he could find her he said. She watched the fog finger the screens. Fog bothered her. She liked the dark.

The dark was rich. But the fog was an intruder. You could see it coming for one thing. The dark came like the dawn seeping into and through the sky's palette. It was a regular thing. Fog was a leak. The dark was dependable. A woman could shut out the dark by turning on a light or just let it be and sit there in the dark thinking things and watching what the dark could do to the sea. The dark could be stopped by a candle. The fog shut you in - it penetrated, it made the air thick and still and it could not be stopped with headlights or even the strobe of a light house.

Toullaine gasped. She realized she wasn't breathing. *What a weird thing to do.* She got up. She went in the house and dialed Jerry the Fisherman. It always took a while for him to answer the phone so she waited.

"H'lo?" Jerry's voice came from some place faraway in him.

Toullaine asked him if he could see anything in this *soup.*

"Nope."

"Lynne Doddie headed out there 15 minutes ago."

"You can't fish," Jerry said.

"Yeah, but you seen her?"

"I ain't seen nuthin'."

Something in *seen nuthin'* got Toullaine's ear. Getting Jerry to talk was like prying a clam open.

"You hear somethin', Jerry?"

"Motorcycle. It's makin' a racket."

"Right now?" Toullaine was paying attention.

The snarl of a motorcycle blasted out of the receiver. Jerry must have been holding it out for her to hear. Toullaine pulled it off her ear.

"You hear that?"

"Yeah. It's loud. Who is it?"

"Keeps riding up my drive. It's in my yard. I got my gun."

"Jerry, don't do anything." The line went quiet. "Jerry?"

"It stopped," Jerry said.

"What?"

"The motorcycle. It stopped. See."

He must have been holding the phone out again. There was dead quiet on the line. Toullaine was bothered. When she got the vision of the red head on the motorcycle, she wasn't sure. But her visions always took time to percolate.

"I'm going out there."

He meant the fog. "Jerry?"

"Yeah?"

"Leave the phone - off the hook."

Toullaine heard the receiver hit the table in Jerry's front room. Then she heard the creak of the screen door and the soft whack as it came to again - then boots on gravel - then nothing. She waited. There was grey fog up against every window and door in her house. It was like she painted it that color. She grabbed a mug off a hook and poured herself some coffee. It'd been on the stove all day reheating and was pretty stiff. She took a swallow. It stung her throat. She looked at the kitchen clock red on the wall. It was 8:01. There was a Reader's Digest on the counter. She fingered the pages then dropped it in the trash. Her nails needed doing. Lynne was good at nails. Boots on gravel - Toullaine was pretty sure she heard it. She waited. Then the soft whack of the screen door. She waited a second or two more before she knew the way she sometimes knew things that there was somebody on the other end of the line that wasn't Jerry. Toullaine didn't move - she didn't breathe.

Some music came on, but far-off, not at Jerry's but maybe from a car radio passing by outside except nobody with sense would be out on a night like this - *except Lynne Doddie*. Toullaine pressed

72

the receiver into her ear trying to hear harder. There was somebody singing. She tried to make it out - *those leet-tle eyes so help-less* something-something- something *flash and send you crash-ing...*

Toullaine knew Maurice Chevalier when she heard it. When she was a kid in her Dad's act, that's what they played on the loudspeaker when she came on - *thank hea-van for leet-tle girls.* She was a little pink ball of fluff and magic her Mother said. Her Dad said she had IT and Toullaine knew she did. At 4, 5, and 6 years old, she'd run out into the ring and the sound of the paying customers cheering would rise up and she'd grab hold of the hoist - one leg in, one leg extended and up she'd go - *without them what would leet-tle boys do - thank hea-va-n thank hea-van-n thank hea-van.* If Toullaine believed in coincidence, she probably would have figured Chevalier singing to her from far-off on a foggy night for coincidence. But Toullaine learned early in life that nothing was coincidence and she was pissed off somebody was playing her like this.

"What is this? Memory lane?" Her voice croaked.

It was quiet as fog on the line.

"Hey, Red! I'd like to speak to my pal, Jerry! You got that?"

The voice on the other end when it came sounded miked - it had static in it like an old 78 rpm record: "Then I better come get ya', huh."

Toot

There was a big bank of fog out on the peninsula. It was reaching for the moon. *So what.* She wasn't showing up. All he could think was what he'd tell Bill. *I decided to stay home - watch the Phillies.* Right. Bill recognized her after she turned around - but by then, it was too late - Toot was already on it. Maybe he could say that - that she was Bill's girl - that he had a pang of conscience. Toot had enough of waiting. He'd been standing in the bayberry bushes too long. He headed out across the field towards the parking lot wondering what Ginny was doing and cursing blonds. Girls drove him nuts. *Especially strawberry blonds.* He heard the metallic click just before a motion light washed out the dark and lit up his end of the parking lot. He stopped. He thought about playing with it - stepping back and forth making it go *clickety-click*. He found out he could do that 2 summers ago. Then he showed Bill. One night the two of them got this one light going on-off on-off on-off clickety-click and then it got stuck and did an all night hiccup. Then something went wrong in the circuit and all the motion lights started doing it. *It was too much. It looked like a disco.* All those summer people calling up the chief telling him to do something - the parking lot was blinking like the rides on the boardwalk. Toot decided maybe he should get a regular girl in town - forget about Ginny and strawberry blond pleasure bunnies that were way out of his reach.

Nothin's out of my reach.

That's what he thought he said out loud and then he tripped some more motion lights and the parking lot came on like a stadium lit up for a night game and right in the middle - dead center - looking like the best deal on a used car lot was the baby blue Chevrolet convertible.

Toot almost whooped. She was there all the time! He started running. He couldn't believe it! *whoa - chill out* Toot pulled himself together - downshifted into a straight walk, flipped his leather jacket back over his left shoulder hooking it with his left thumb and swiped the sweat off his lip with his right pointy finger.

She was asleep in the back seat stretched out strawberry blond and oh so pretty. *Gees - what a girl.* He wanted to get in there with her, just slide in the backseat and get in there. He looked around the parking lot. It was September and the moon was full. The summer crowd was gone. The town was getting back to normal. The chief wouldn't be cruising out here tonight. There was nothing to stop him. Toot opened the door on the passenger side. It made a thump. She didn't move - not a stir. Girls did that - they pretended to be asleep. Toot knew this because of a woman out on Mermaid Lane. He was painting her shutters on Tuesdays - summer of 10th grade - there was a *slew* of them. She drove him nuts walking back and forth inside the windows and sliders with nothing on but a yellow T-shirt - no panties. And then this one Tuesday, he comes inside to get his money and she's asleep on the couch with her T-shirt riding up on her thighs showing her snatch. Toot took it for what it was. He made some preliminary moves and she woke up all flushed and hot and so surprised *like what'd she think was gonna' happen.* He got on her and she liked it and so did he and then it was a regular Tuesday thing until September. She didn't come back the next summer.

Toot didn't know for sure if this was like that. *Girls sleep.* Maybe this one got tired of waiting for him just like he got tired of waiting for her but she didn't want to leave on the chance he might show up. Toot let himself feel bad for her waiting here all by herself in the dark. Then he got in.

It was a tight fit in the backseat with her sprawled out on her side but he could squeeze in alongside on the floor. She was breathing regular in and out. Maybe she was asleep. Her breasts were pushing at the buttons on her blouse - in and out in and out. Toot felt turned-on. He could see skin under the knot of her shirttails - a thin line of it just above her black stretch pants.

"Hey." He said it soft.

Too soft - she didn't stir.

He hesitated then he put his hand on the side of her hip. *Nuthin'.* He took his thumb and strummed the side of her tummy. She sighed. And Toot's heart flipped over. *whoa* He checked the parking lot out her rear window, then took a look out the right side one then the left and out the windshield too. It was quiet. Every move he made sounded loud to him. And his right foot was screwed up sideways on the hump. Then the motion lights blinked out and he was in the dark for a second and then there was moonlight all over her. *gees* She was something to look at. He touched the skin under her shirttails. He ran a finger under the elastic at the top of her stretch pants. She didn't move but he was pretty sure she stopped breathing. *Okay, baby, this the way you want it - I'm into it.* He pushed his hand down inside and found her belly button - *oh man* - she had an outy. He ran two of his fingers as soft as he could around and around and around her belly button all the time watching her pretty face. *Come on, do something, wake up!* Toot knew what he wanted to do. He wanted to get the pants out of the way and push his tongue into the soft nub of flesh in the center of the belly button. She moaned.

That about made Toot stand up but he bonked his head hard on the steel brace that held up the canvas roof of her car and twisted his pelvis coming down hard sideways on his right side *fuck*. He was cramping up and it hurt like hell and all of a sudden he was tired of girls who wanted it but wouldn't show it - like Ginny - and *fuck this* he wasn't *fucking no corpse.* Toot felt like crying but he wouldn't do that. He pushed her pants down out of the way - there were freckles all over - and then he was staring at her gold - her pussy was a sparkling bush of gold in the moonlight. Toot loved pussy - he couldn't help it - pussy got him every time. Toot got up on his knees pulling at his fly.

"Hey, come on - wake up, baby!" He was pleading with her - *shit* - he didn't even know her name.

He opened up his pants. Then he reached under her and pulled her pants down off her to her knees. She still wasn't moving. She wasn't moving. He registered that fact.

Why isn't she moving?

And then he heard the blast of the Harley cutting down the Boulevard coming at him from the sea. He couldn't see it. And then the motion lights came on again in a explosion of glare and he still couldn't see it but the noise was making his ears ring - it was splitting them open! It hurt! The sound went round and round snarling and spitting everywhere he turned.

"STOPIT - FUCK - STOPIT, MAN!"

Toot was holding onto his ears. It struck him that maybe in that split second - in that awful ripping sound, he'd lost his hearing. He lifted his palms off. He didn't want that sound back. His ears stopped ringing. Then it went quiet. That's what was wrong. It wasn't just her being quiet. There was no insect sounds coming from the field and that went for the whole time he was in the backseat too. No crickets. No katydids.

Nothing.

Toot looked out. There was fog at the edge of the parking lot. *Where'd it come from?* He looked up for the moon. Gone. Then there was a clunk on the front end of the car and he turned to see somebody big straighten up from the bumper. He couldn't see the head. The guy was tall. There were spikes gleaming off his belt. The chest was a mat of hair - red. Through the windshield, Toot watched the guy move ahead into the lot away from the car. His shoulders swelled up and rolled over his neck. His head was sunk behind a bulge of muscle. This guy worked out a lot. Then Toot saw the Harley. It was parked maybe 20 feet out in front of the convertible. It was big and black. It had a gleam in it like a smile. That's what it looked like to Toot - like the Harley was smiling at him. The big guy threw a leg on and when he did, the Harley looked like it'd met its match. That's when Toot saw the tow.

Toot moved fast. He pulled at his zipper and grabbed his jacket. He felt bad leaving her but he figured she was *his* and Toot was no match for this guy. The Harley roared to life. Toot couldn't get the release lever on the front seat to let go. He scrambled over and the gearshift got him in the groin. It didn't matter how much it hurt. He got his hand on the handle of the passenger door and the car lunged forward. Toot got up off the seat and looked out. The big guy was pulling her car with his Harley. He was making a U-ey - clean - in a large arc - heading out to the exit and the fog. Toot jerked the handle. The door swung open and Toot rolled out. He got up on the run.

Jones

Toot could see the field that ran all the way out to bayside and all the big bushes he could hide in coming at him. That's all he had to do - sprint maybe 100 yards more - and nobody could find him. Behind him, Toot heard the Harley drop down to idle. He knew the way through the bushes - only locals knew the way - it was a maze of low dunes and bushes. Toot made it off the asphalt. The Harley couldn't maneuver in the sand. All he had to do was get to the bayberry bushes and he was in. Toot fell. He went down. It was his boots. He should have had sneakers on. The Harley came to life behind him - that sound revving up then exploding across the parking lot on a dead run. Toot got up running. He was flying. His chest burned. He hit sand. And then the Harley was beside him and in front of him and Toot was dodging but it was like the big guy was corralling him, herding him back and back - sand spitting - and every move he made towards the bush was blocked and he found himself on the asphalt running for the car with the Harley up his ass and it just wasn't possible for Toot to get away.

Toullaine

Toullaine was looking up at Barney's blue railroad light. She felt the tracks he'd left on her soul. A buoy sounded out in the fog but it was hard to get the direction. Barney had been a good friend to Toullaine. He'd loved her even after the third miscarriage. She made him go. It was the only time in her life she could remember really being mean. She looked at her hands. They were strong still from the trapeze. *No rings.* She'd had her journey. There was a change in pressure. Barney's blue light spit out. It fizzed, then it spit out. And then - fog. Toullaine wasn't sure what made her get up off the bench and put her hands into the fog. She kept going though until her palms hit canvas. It was Lynne's car. She knew it in a breath. Lynne's favorite scent was *Olio*. She felt down for the handle but the door pushed open. There was a kid in there - she knew him from the supermarket - there wasn't much either one of them could say.

*He felt bad leaving her but he figured she was
his and Toot was no match for this guy.*

"Thanks."

Inside she could see the poor kid was trembling. She pulled the door shut on her side and Lynne's car slid forward. The kid wasn't driving so Toullaine assumed they were being pushed or getting pulled.

"He's towing us with the Harley," the kid said.

"The red head." Toullaine needed the confirmation.

"Yeah, I guess - can't see the head."

Nowhere in her vision had it been revealed to her that the red head was headless. If it turned out to be the case, she was going to a place she'd never been. Toullaine decided to cross that bridge when she came to it. She was a truster of fate.

"It weird, ya' know." The kid was looking straight ahead. "I can't hear it."

"What?"

"The Harley."

Toullaine listened for the hum of a well-tuned engine. She'd spent some time with a biker once. It didn't take long for her to know it was not the life for her, but she'd learned something about engines. The guy she was with was a loner but on Tuesday nights, they'd put in at some garage or other he knew along the way and there'd be a bunch of other bikers there with their women. It was like a corral of Harleys - every bike in its own way a classic. She could remember thinking that it must have been like this in the old country where her grandparents pulled into a closed caravan for the night. She herself had traveled on the circus train. Traveling on the back of that Harley was a space in her life that was outside time or place. It was before Toullaine understood the price of freedom. She listened hard. The kid was right - there was nothing out there but fog.

"Did I ever tell you about the time my brother did a flipover and missed the wire? He was some-thing. My Mother said even greater than my Father. My Father made his reputation in Hungary. It was a small traveling band of performers before my time. In Budapest, he met my Mother. She was a potato grower for her family. Her specialty was onion soup. I can taste it now with my tongue. But if you asked me to make my Mother's onion soup, I would tell you it went to the grave with her. I mean this quite literally. At her death bed, she whispered the ingredients to me - the timing - she had held it back for all those years. She was 68 - a hard life - and so at her order, I wrote it down. And then she took a breath and died. It moved me. At the funeral Mass, I had the recipe in my pocket. I kept reaching into my skirt to make sure it was there. It was the only copy. At the gravesite, I knew it was not mine to keep. So I made them open the coffin. An old man fainted. A woman gasped. My Mother's mouth had snapped the threads of the undertaker's needle. She looked as if she were objecting. I knew I was right. I took the recipe for onion soup from my pocket and placed it in her mouth. I believed my Mother regretted her choice to divulge the ingredients of her onion soup."

The kid was looking at her funny. "What about your brother?"

"Ah. That's a story worth telling. My Father was a trapeze artist. He was squat and small. Every fiber of him was muscle. He breathed the circus. This was my hope - to be like my Father. I was young no more than 6 when it happened but already my body held the strength of a true trapeze artist. My Mother was a fortune teller. She made up things she said and moved the cards around and told people back their dreams. But that day in her tent in the side show - no matter what she did - the death card found its way to the top of her deck. People re-cog-nize the death card no matter how fast your hands move. It isn't good for business. My brother was fourteen. He was not built like my Father. He was long limbed like my Mother."

The kid was with her now. He'd stopped trembling. His eyes were huge. A good looking kid. His physique was mature. Whatever was coming, he was involved. He'd need his wits. So would Toullaine.

"There was in the circus at that time a woman who pretended to be a man. She wore a scarf to hide the fact that she had no Adam's apple. She wore the clothes of an organ grinder - a vest and baggy pants. She wore a mustache - bushy brown that curled down by her chin. And on her head a squashed fedora with a yellow band. I'd watch her in the mirror watch herself become the man. She worked with a small hand organ - the kind you wind like a jack-in-the box and she had a monkey too. I enjoyed her act but my brother loved it. She'd enter the wire casually as if she hadn't expected to walk there. Then she'd make a sweeping bow to the audience and wind her organ as if that is what they came to hear - her to play the organ. The tune was like the hurdy-gurdy on the carousel - it was repetitious and struck the same notes over and over as she traveled with her monkey out on the wire. The monkey on the other hand was not so casual. She convinced him by training him to act scared when they hit the wire. The little thing would look down and screech and run back to the safety of the perch. And she would bow and wind her organ and oh so casually with her head nod him out onto the wire - as if there were nothing to fear. And so the act became the organ grinder convincing the monkey to cross the wire with her. In the middle, the monkey would become so frantic; he would grab onto her crotch and she would lift her feet - one up - the other up - in mock pain for mock testicles then she did a handstand and still the monkey held onto her crotch and the paying customers would go crazy with laughter. And that just made the monkey wilder screeching its objections all the way... But at last the organ grinder with the casual grace of one who knows would convince the little fellow - he had a cap with a bell on it - to balance on the wire holding a small orange and red umbrella above his little monkey face in his little monkey hand. You could hear a pin drop as the little monkey overcame its fear. And when they reached the opposite perch, the crowd would applaud and cry out *bravo*. And the monkey would bow. And the organ grinder would bow. You don't see acts like that in the circus any more."

Toullaine had shifted in her seat turning to face her audience. The rhythms of her native tongue came back with the stories and soothed her and the boy from the supermarket. Lynne Doddie was laid out on the back seat. Toullaine took a start.

"She's okay. She's breathing okay." The boy was looking at Lynne with regret. "I was meetin' her and then there she was like this."

Toullaine thought he'd cry. "It's okay, kid. Just trust what is hap-pen-ing and keep a lookout for the alternative."

Lynne's car turned and dropped off the asphalt. Both of them felt the soft crunch of gravel underneath the tires. Toullaine wondered for a second why the kid didn't make a run for it but watching him she could see he was beginning to believe the magic. It was no good if this boy believed he could not get away. It was no good. Something at the edge of her mind warned her for the boy. Her visions, when they came, were sometimes mirages. They'd show up on the sliders off her deck. In a tidal pool. On a blank TV screen. But in the fog, where could she find the place for her reflection? Toullaine looked on the dashboard and then out at the side view mirror. *No mirrors*. Toullaine wouldn't work with mirrors. A drop of water rolled out of her nose. She swiped at it. Blood. Red. Toullaine touched the blood on her thumb with her finger - a single drop. This was a harbinger - an omen. Toullaine needed a place to be - so her body had room to experience her vision. She needed to calm herself - to let it come to her. And she needed a witness and this kid was it maybe – maybe not - *what's he doin' here?* Not that a soul would believe him but somebody might come out here and poke around and find what Toullaine was beginning to dread.

"Hokus-pokus, kid."

Jerry the Fisherman

One thing about being in a box, it gave a man time to think. The only things he kept in here were lobster traps in winter and sometimes nets. He wasn't ready yet to move them up from the beach. He didn't fish himself anymore. He was fished out. He made a living stuffing fish for men who believed it was the size of the fish they caught giving them the satisfaction. He liked his regulars. The guy from the Poconos with the rain gear especially. He caught a 22 pound blue fish a summer ago with a flat spoon Jerry had for bait. Skyrocketed out of the sea and the Pocono guy got him. Jerry enjoyed stuffing that fish.

Then there was the weird looking mutt that came with the doctor from Pennsylvania. He liked to follow Jerry around. Stand with him at the helm.

Funny.

Jerry the Fisherman was locked inside his storage box by the side of the shed. All he could see in the openings in the slats was the fog. His old bones were settling for the cramped position he was in - not so painful now as at first. Jerry almost didn't know what hit him he landed in here so fast. *Something big.* People in town always said he shouldn't live alone out by the lighthouse but Jerry was ready. He'd always been ready. And up until tonight, nothing had ever happened to him that Jerry considered a problem. Including this - once he got out of it - because he was always ready.

He drifted back to thinking - of this woman - came up here with her husband - brought a big thermos full of martinis she'd drink. Her husband didn't drink - he fished. They'd hire Jerry's boat just for them. She'd go up on the foredeck and get pretty drunk. Jerry made them sign a waiver that if she fell off, it wasn't his fault. *Happy to do it.*

There.

He got it. The third screw that held the hinge to the top on the right side dropped into the sand. Jerry pushed at it. It gave a little but the clamp on the front was still holding the top down. Jerry sighed. Then he turned over on his side, pushed himself with his foot to the other end of the storage box, and inserted his jackknife into the first screw that held the other hinge in place.

Toot

Toot knew what she was doing. The fortune-teller lady was trying to get him to feel better. But she wasn't almost run down by the Harley now, was she? It was nice though. He rubbed his chest. His pectoral muscles felt sore.

His Mom went to this lady - he couldn't remember her name. She told his Mom she was done with what she came to do - she told her she could go. Toot was in 6th grade he remembered. And then, that night, while they were eating TV dinners - fried chicken - his favorite - every time he looked up, his Mom was watching him. If he traced it back, that's when it started - his Mom watching him. The night of the fortune teller lady. Like he was a little kid or something. Like it was the last time she was seeing him. *Yeah, like that.*

"We're here." The fortune teller was looking out the windshield.

Toot felt the convertible roll to a stop. Then the door on the driver's side opened and the big guy yanked him out by the collar of his pressed leather jacket. He had to scramble to get his feet under him. Then he was getting pushed along the drive. He tried to turn around and see but the big guy kept slapping him on the back of his neck. Then a car door slammed and he heard from behind him the fortune teller lady call out.

"Hey - you!"

Is she kidding? Toot wanted to smile but the back of his neck hurt. Then the fortune teller caught up going as fast as she could. *She's crazy.* This guy was big. She was breathing hard but she matched them step for step. Toot glanced over. She was lookin' straight ahead - not at Toot - not at the big guy - just straight ahead. She was determined - he had to give her that.

"Jerry?!" She yelled it out. "Jerry!"

A boot in the small of his back kept Toot on the move.

"Jerry! Call out if you can!"

"Toullaine?" The voice was weak but it was nearby.

"You okay?" The fortune teller was relieved - Toot could hear it in her voice.

It had to be Jerry the Fisherman's place. Toot hadn't been out here since he stopped skinning fish for Jerry when he was 12. Jerry was old then.

Again the boot in the small of his back but this time Toot got *pissed*.

"Cut it the fuck out! You hear me?! Cut it the-"

A big meaty fist caught him in the side of his mouth and Toot fell down. And then there was something loose in his mouth and blood and he spit a tooth into his hand.

"Don't talk." It was the fortune teller. "Don't talk to it."

The big guy was coming at him - and Toot tried to get up - but out of nowhere something hit him on the top of his head and knocked him down flat in the sand.

Jerry the Fisherman

Jerry managed to unscrew the second hinge and push the top off the storage box. He heard the clamp on the front go *kaput* as it went down. Then Toullaine was coming at him out of the fog. He saw her before she saw him. Then she smacked into the side of the box and almost fell in there with him.

"Jerry?"

"Yeah. It's me, Toullaine." He gave her a push back.

"Hey!" The voice was outside the box.

"Kid?" Toullaine was looking around.

"Get offa' me."

Toullaine stepped off the lid of the storage box and a kid Jerry used to know was underneath it. All this was a lot for Jerry to take in. He wanted to get out of the storage box but wasn't so sure he could get his leg over.

The kid shoved the lid back off of himself. "Where's the guy? Where'd he go?"

"Shhhh." Toullaine said.

The three of them stood there listening to the fog.

Surf then - a car door getting slammed.

"That's weird." Toullaine was looking back in the direction of the road.

"What?" was the kid.

"Why would it care?"

Then somethin' - sound of boots squashing sound out of sand.

"What's your name?" Toullaine was asking the kid.

"What?"

"Your given name - quick."

"They call me Toot, lady."

Jerry knew all about the kid's name. He remembered the kid in the summers hating it when his buddies showed up after a full day of mackerels or blues. They'd call it out from over the dunes. It was just a name but he hated it. Toullaine wouldn't ask if she didn't need it.

"Yeshua," Jerry said. "Yeshua ben Yosef.

"Ah – don't. Gimme' a break."

Toullaine was looking hard at the kid.

"Josh-u-a," said the kid. "My name's Joshua."

"Je-sus," said Toullaine.

Toullaine

It fell in place like a brick. This was the kid of the woman who came out to see her on a hot night in August 4 summers back. No - it was longer ago than that. It was late at night. The surf was still. It was after a hurricane. The beaches were clean. But the ocean was still. It shouldn't have been. Toullaine wondered about that at the time. The woman had been drinking - not much - just enough. Beer. When she spoke, her voice was feminine. Soft. Like the night.

She didn't understand her life she said. It was meaningless to her. Toullaine told her nothing was meaningless. The woman said she liked the sea - the sound. She was looking out the sliders behind the couch. Toullaine was struck by that because the ocean that night was so still. She had a iridescent scarf on her head tied at the nape of her neck and a perfect profile. It was hard not to stare at her. She said she came here after a man - a seminarian out of Jersey City - she was 16 - he was 24 - she said - when she came. He said this town was where his people came from. She said before that - she was thinking of joining the novitiate. She said - she was raised in an orphanage by the Missionary Sisters of the Sacred Heart of Jesus. Toullaine remembered that. She said she came to this place instead. In the glass sliders behind the woman, Toullaine had a flash - she saw a magician's silver handkerchief shimmer before it got whipped away to reveal an A-frame house up on blocks with its chimney going. It looked like a picture somebody would take with a Brownie camera except there was a storm hovering over the house - angry blue clouds and black night. A yellow light was on in the back room. That and the chimney smoke. And then the hot August night resurfaced in Toullaine's sliders and the house in the dunes was gone. There was somebody else beside the woman hiding in that house. *hiding* Toullaine remembered thinking that word - *hiding*.

"You live alone?" Toullaine watched the woman turn and run her slender fingers along the fabric on the back of the couch.

"No. With my son."

"Leave him. You can go." Toullaine found herself saying. "What you came to do is done."

"He's twelve," said the woman - her eyes held such longing, "He's only twelve."

Toullaine watched the kid's face - a rough cut but good looking. He had big hands. His shoulders were nubs of muscle. He was skinny but in shape. His mouth was sensual. His eyes were alert - on the prowl. When he turned, he had his Mother's profile. Toullaine took it all in because she understood now.

I'm the witness.

The kid was helping Jerry out of the crate. Jerry was more fragile than Toullaine was used to thinking about him. She took that in. The kid was looking up and past her. Toullaine turned around just as the red head came out of the fog. Lynne was wrapped around its fat neck. Toullaine wondered what it did to Lynne to put her out like that.

"Why don't you leave her alone? She didn't do nuthin'." The kid seemed a little taller to Toullaine - she noticed how he separated himself out from her and Jerry.

"Hrrr-r"- that's what it sounded like - came out of the red head's mouth with a wad of spit. *No eyes - goggles.*

A fog horn blew three short blasts. The red head lifted up its nose and sniffed. *Like a pig.* Then he turned with Lynne into the fog. Toullaine knew what she had to do and was grateful when the kid and Jerry followed along.

The red head was on the move up ahead - the three of them had to scramble. Lynne would say he was moving like Schwarzenegger in *The Terminator*. Toullaine had a pang - she wanted Lynne to make it through this night. *Please, God.* Jerry was falling behind.

"Go 'awn. Keep up. I'll find ya'."

The dunes rolled around Jerry's part of the peninsula dipping down, climbing back up. There was low scrub everywhere and more than once Toullaine felt the sting of thorns pricking her ankles. The red head was a blue shadow maybe 20 feet ahead in the fog. But there was a difference now that they were getting so close to the ocean. Toullaine could hear the surf *loud and clear* and there was wind stirring the soup around, lifting it up, whisking it off.

Toullaine and the kid were in a sort of ravine where several dunes swept down - they'd been following the redhead *pretty close* but all of a sudden, he was gone.

"Beat that. Where'd he go?" The kid was surveying the tops of the dunes.

The fog was lifting - there was some light in the sky behind the gossamer. It was deep and blue. The kid was breathing beside her - nice and even now - which was more than she could say for herself.

"He doesn't know her." It came out of him like a burst.

Toullaine waited.

"He doesn't know her. And he doesn't give s-shit"

"Lynne - you mean," Toullaine said.

"I don't know who I am."

"Nobody knows who they are, kid - not even Einstein."

"Yeah, but I feel like I should know - like I could make it all different - if I know. Like if it wasn't for me, he never woulda' got her."

Toullaine thought of Lynne's dream. *Bait.* It was a premonition. That's what it was. Lynne was in tune with herself - she paid attention to the signs. People didn't do that so much anymore. But Lynne did. She sensed it coming but could it be that it was sucking her energy transmuting her into its web? *Bait.* Toullaine looked up at the confusion in the boy's eyes.

"Maybe you're just a regular kid named Jesus. Maybe that's it. Maybe all we have to do is get Lynne out of this."

"Yeah."

Toot

The roar of a hundred Harleys or it seemed like that to him exploded out of the sky like a 21 gun salute and then there they were flying - up and out of the dunes into the night on a projection that dropped them down through the dissolving fog into the ravine landing in a near perfect order of circular pounce.

Toot had his hands over his ears. They all looked like vultures to him. One leg tweaked out on a scratch, shoulders balled up, fat fists keying their machines, small bald heads. That's what scared him most. They were mindless. He could see that. Their control was coming from someplace deeper than instinct.

jesusjesusjesusjesusjesusjesusjesusjesusjesusjesusjesusjesus

It was in the snarl of the engines - his name over and over and he knew he heard it. He felt the fortune teller shift behind him. He didn't turn to watch her. He waited for her to come into his peripheral vision.

She had on a muumuu and a worn-out sweater. It was brown with flecks of green. But when she raised up her arms - she looked like a prophet or a picture of a prophet - like Moses on the hill with a bunch of people down below - *the golden calf.* Toot didn't want to believe in God. He didn't want to believe in giving it up to anybody. When it came down to it, it was just *him.* And - his *mom.*

Jones

"Did I ever tell you about the time - my brother did a flip-over - and missed the wire?!"

Toot couldn't stop his mouth from twitching into a smile so he pulled his upper lip in under his teeth and then he couldn't believe it - because from the time these guys showed up, they'd been revving their engines and the sound was bad - it hurt like thunder - but then a word from her and it all stopped. Toot watched as biker after biker shut down his machine and *jesus* stopped ringing like rap in his ears.

"When my brother was fifteen, I was a girl of six. We traveled by train from city to city with our parents and their small but specialized one ring circus..."

And then he was alone in his head in the dunes with the lull of her voice like the surf underneath. His job was to get out. His job was to *get away.* A part of him wanted to cry but he shut it off into a part of his mind he wasn't going to again. He knew the fortune teller would hold the bikers for as long as she could but if the mind that ran them worked like his, she had 5 minutes, maybe a little more, before it came to. He'd listened in the Chevy to her talk; she'd only held him to the seat in the bit about the onion soup. *Maybe longer - monkey man.*

Jerry the Fisherman

Jerry was in the third tunnel - the one that cut through the dunes that backed into the beach. Usually he didn't trust this particular tunnel. It was old. There was orange rust and water dripping down and wind ran through it like a whip. He could see the blue in the dark at the end. He had his flashlight. He made himself speed up. It was clearing. They were losing the fog. Toullaine said it would come down to this - the two of them against *fortune?* Jerry never knew what *the heck* she meant. On Saturday nights, she'd come out here and they'd play gin rummy and drink hot cider and towards the end, she'd repeat it - *it's us against fortune, Jerry.*

At the ladder, Jerry climbed up into the tube that ran up to the top of the last dune. It was dark inside here but dryer and a tight fit. He slipped on a rung but saved himself. The knuckles in his right hand hurt. So did his knees and ankles. Jerry didn't mind old age as much as some but tonight he could have used some dexterity.

At the top, he inserted his special L key and pushed. The cover lifted up like a garbage can lid. Jerry installed these tops after a tourist who shouldn't have been out here fell in one of the tunnels. There was a wind and as he climbed up and out, Jerry could see a dark blue sky riding by in the patches in the fog.

Toot

Toot made himself still. He let his eyes work around the circle. The bikers at any given spot were fifteen feet back from him and the fortune teller. That might give him a second or two - tops. It was time to move.

"Balesford was my brother's elephant - not so large as Kingbutte or Queen Bathilde but better - more adept in the ring..."

Toot walked easy on a direct line towards the biker directly in front of him. The sea was on the other side of the big dunes. He knew it from all his summers out here. He played tag ball here and King of the Hill and when he was by himself - *shells*. Something was making his mind slow up and his eyes lose focus. He felt himself staring back into the maze of time.

"And the monkey woman helped my brother to coax Balesford across the bridge. Balesford was reluctant, we all thought, because the bridge was narrow and high but my Mother watching upon her return from Budapest where her own dear Mother was taken with the influenza shook her head in that way that mothers have and took my Father aside..."

Toot brought himself back. The fortune teller's voice receded. He was looking in the eyes of the one biker. It was impossible to know if the biker was looking back on account of the goggles. The one biker and the 2 guys to either side had on black goggles. And for a second Toot got the sensation that the goggles were the eyes and that he was a distortion trapped inside like a mirror in the fun house. The three of them also had red spiked balding hair. They were alike. They were exactly alike. Toot knew if he looked around the circle, all the others would be the same. It was like he walked into his own nightmare.

When he was little when he woke up scared in the night - too scared even to turn on the light - it was the sound of Harleys he heard revving in his head making him sick with their thunder. And he'd lie there watching the dark sheet of sky in his window waiting for one of them to crash through it but then, they'd pass by - he'd hear them going down the Boulevard - and he'd go back to sleep. But when he got to be twelve, he felt his time. It came up. He asked his Mom if he could switch bedrooms with her. The window in her room looked out on a dune of sea grass. He could watch the moon cross the sky in there. And his Mom said okay. And they worked for a week. And the nightmare didn't come back.

"I can say that in this one thing - my Father was a fool - for he too loved the monkey woman..."

Her words were like zingers in his head reminding him to keep going. There was no clean break through. The right leg of each biker held to a footrest - the other leg - the left one - was flexed out on a scratch - boots sinking into the sand under the next bike. The muscular arms of the bikers reached out - one to the throttle - one to the clutch. It was a wall of red muscle and they weren't budging - not even a muscle. Toot took a step forward and placed each one of his hands firmly on a bicep.

"The monkey woman believed they were alone in the arena. I could tell this by the way she touched my brother - she held him steady from behind with the palm of her left hand pressing into his chest. But I was there all the time under the seats watching -

waiting for my brother who had whispered to me in the night that today was the day he would tame the high wire..."

All Toot had to do was pull his feet up on the front tires of 2 bikes and he'd have the leverage he wanted to push himself up and over. He needed to calm his solar plexus. He listened for the fortune teller. There was a pause in the air. *Where is she?* And then he heard.

She was sobbing - bub-bub-bubbing in the middle of the ring of bikers - like a crybaby - *shit!*

Then up against the sky at the top of the dune was Jerry the Fisherman like a scarecrow waving in the wind and Toot lifted his knees and swung up in-between and over and was down grabbing his balance out of the sand and running full tilt to the top of the dune.

Jerry the Fisherman

Jerry didn't wait for Toot. He scrambled down the far side of the dune as fast as his old bones would let him. He knew the kid would catch up and halfway down Toot did. He caught Jerry in the armpit and lifted him up from what would have been a head- on fall. It was great having the kid's energy feed him and for that brief run, Jerry remembered it was good to be alive.

Jerry had a catamaran and 2 dinghies with small motors attached further down the beach but as he led Toot to them, he was having doubts about which to use. The dinghies could maneuver the waterways through the grasslands. The catamaran would take the wind and fly around the point. If the fog wasn't lifting off, Jerry'd pick the dinghy. There was cover in the grasslands - and the waterways cut through the peninsula on a more direct heading for the bay. With the fog and Jerry's knowledge of the inland, nobody would find them. He looked out. There was wind whipping up the water from the northeast. It was hard sailing into that. Jerry was an old man - his strength was gone. Catamarans were for boys and middle-aged fools. Toot ran on ahead. He was at the catamaran pushing it off its slider. Behind him half hidden in the fog, one of the dinghies was off its stops, at the edge of the water, rocking each time the surf rolled in. Jerry didn't like it. He secured all his equipment up the beach off the tideline after a fishing party. *No way it got loose.* Jerry passed the catamaran and got to it.

Lynne Doddie was lying on her back *nekid* in the dinghy. Jerry shut his eyes and remembered Palermo - *Jesus - all those years- all those years - it coulda' been me and Wanda - all those years.*

Toot was standing on the other side of the dinghy. He was looking down at Lynne Doddie like she was his. He took off his jacket and lifted her up and put it on her and water seeped out of her mouth on a trickle and Toot pulled her jaw down and put his mouth over hers and after what seemed like a long time, her chest convulsed and she kicked out and she was choking and coughing and water was pouring out of her like puke and the surf rolled in more powerful now and lifted the dinghy and pulled it out and Jerry got in and pulled the cord on the motor while Toot ran alongside pushing the dinghy, lifting it up onto the surf into the waves and the sun hit the horizon like a line of electricity under the fog.

Beyond the waves, the motor came to and Jerry took hold of the rudder and steered her around to port. On the water, the fog was thicker. *Good thing.* All he had was 2 horsepower. They needed the cover. He watched Toot sit Lynne up in his arms. Her head was lolling around but she was alive. Jerry wondered how long she'd been in the dinghy like that. He wondered at her being alive too. This whole experience was like a booby trap to Jerry from the minute he put the phone down talking to Toullaine. The water was choppy and the wind was against them. Better the dingy, then, except they were skidding sideways across the water. The dinghy wanted to turn around and go the other way. But Jerry held the rudder to port and the dinghy pulled out of the skid and headed north. He needed to make the cove.

Lynne Doddie was lying on her back nekid *in the dinghy.*

Jones

Once inside he could pick his way through to the bay and no motorcycle was following him in there.

Toullaine

She had never told the story that was only her brother's to tell. In its way, it was like her Mother's recipe for onion soup. She danced around that time when she spun her stories - she used it like a lure - it held her audience to their seats. It was a reference point but she never told how it happened - only the results - *he fell from the high wire, ladies and gen-tle-mens - he was my big brother and he was - dead.* It was okay when she told it like this - skipping the part - the part that led to the fall - the part that was personal - the part that was his seduction and defeat. It still hung in her mind's eye - that final moment of clarity between them. What she saw in his fall - when their eyes for the briefest instant locked - was her brother's sure knowledge that evil had scuttled his ambition for triumph. In the end, he'd been *had.*

They were all sobbing now - every red-headed one of them *like big babies.* Toullaine traversed the circle with her eyes watching their bald beady heads sink into their thick necks. As she turned, they seemed like customers going around on a Round-up. She hoped she could scuttle them - slam them back into zero gravity - leave them hanging there helpless - like her brother. She imagined she could hear the organ grinding the music of the monkey woman somewhere in her left ear - *so far off* - and it made her want to tell these demons what she never even told her Mother.

"Whatever the monkey woman communicated to my brother in that moment in the big tent, I cannot tell. I watched his chest fill and square."

badeda-badeda

It was nonsense growing in her ear - she couldn't really hear it - but it was somehow there and she could see clearly, in her mind's eye, the monkey playing the organ from his perch for her brother.

98

badeda-badeda-badeda-badeda

Always before it was the monkey woman grinding the organ but that time it was the monkey - his little hand a craw on the grinder.

"My brother folded the balls of his left foot gently around the wire and it shot shine along its distance and then back at my brother and was still. This is the way in the circus - the elements coming together to make magic. It does not happen alone for any one."

The red heads were so still. No movement. No sound escaped them. Had she succeeded in holding them? Forever? The surf was pounding beyond the dune. Could she run?

I can still run.

"I knew my brother's power - I saw it emerge in practice with my Father. His concentration was intense - he could become equal to his body as he lifted its form into the handstand on the swinging trapeze. He was long - impossibly long - and languorous. His effect was like slow motion on the screen. What he did seemed deliberate yet impossible. But still my Father held him down away from the green of the limelight. My brother's work with the monkey woman began, I believe, because my brother understood his time would never come under the tutelage of my Father."

badeda-badeda-badeda-badeda

"I pushed myself closer into a crevice between 2 rows of slats in the empty galleria and for a brief moment, I thought the monkey woman's eyes flicked into mine."

But, no. If she knew I was there, she would have resented my presence. She'd intended this feast just for herself. She would not have gone on.

Toullaine had argued with herself about this her whole life. Had the monkey woman known she was there watching? She didn't have the answer.

There was a sound. Close by. Toullaine looked up. The Harleys seemed closer. *But, no.* It was the same.

"My brother was out on the wire. He lowered his poised and bare arms to his sides. In the dark blue air of the big top, he was an angel of light. And so - he clowned on the wire. He bounced like a bad boy on his Mama's bed. And the wire for its part stayed with him moving in counterpoint in the air up and down up and down - *badeda badeda* - like the softest whip. And then he lifted himself higher separating himself from the wire and each time he dropped down from his ascent, the wire was there in the dark blue air rebounding and they met like friends - my brother and the wire - like partners - and the monkey woman laughed and applauded their precision."

"Something came and got my attention. I recall looking at the post that held the monkey's perch that led out to the wire. There was the faintest rapping - regular like my brother's bounce and then it stopped. When I looked back, the wire was still. My brother was preparing for the backward flipover. It is a difficult move on a wire. My brother had done it in practice. But he had done it with a net. There was no net that day. In performance, the monkey woman like my Father refused the net. It is illegal in the circus now - but then it held the audience to their seats."

A Harley snarled.

Toullaine stopped.

She felt her breaths shallow and quick in her mouth. She could hold them with her brother's story - *more* - she must hold them with her brother's story. And then another Harley - in back of her this time - snarled. Toullaine turned around as they each - every single red-headed one of them - dropped their right boot down from the bike into the sand and rolled ever so slightly forward. Toullaine felt transfixed. She had never known fear - she had always gone forward - from the time of her brother's death - she was a truster of fate.

"My brother sent his arms extending out in front of him - a perfect right angle to his chest."

The Harleys stopped.

"My brother looked back over his shoulder; the monkey woman nodded. Then my brother looked down at the ring - and - then - with his mouth relaxed into the ironic smile that was only his - I held my breath..."

Toullaine could feel it coming up inside her and wished *please* for her brother to be with her here now. *Oh, God, please, let Miksa be with me now.*

Toullaine turned and searched the tops of the dunes. The sky had the early reach of sunrise in it - a gold and pink stroke of genius killing the miasma in the fog. It was so welcome Toullaine said *ahh.* Then the heat of the Harleys reached her.

"...and in that split time - when my brother lifted his body into an aerial curl - I heard the jamb that held the pulley that controlled the high wire tension lift out of its slot and I saw it drop and drop to the floor and I looked up to see the monkey screaming and my brother twisting in the dark blue air seeking his landing and the wire pulling pulling like a careless ribbon out of its anchor and the bright blueness of his eyes disbelieving the falling wire as he lunged in thin air trying to catch at it and almost not missing it and falling and he fell and he fell - and in that brief second, found my eyes with his smile - and landed on his back."

Jerry the Fisherman

He was in the drawbridge house drinking coffee out of Toullaine's coffee maker. Jerry knew she was gone. He knew when it happened. It was like a light went out. Toot was out on the bridge - pacing. It was sunrise. Lynne was weak - sprawled out on the daybed Toullaine used in-between boats. When this was a fishing town, there was traffic for this bridge but in the years that made it a summer place, having a bridge watch in the middle of the night was almost a waste of time. They'd replace the bridge Jerry knew with a super causeway lifted up on pilings out of the way of mainsails. People like Jerry and Toullaine weren't useful any more.

"Here she comes." It was Toot.

Jerry put his coffee cup down and went out on the bridge to watch a jeep approach. The sun was behind it blinking out his view of the driver. Jerry put his hand up to see. The jeep stopped and a woman got out. Jerry figured it was Toot's mother. She was younger than he was expecting.

"I'll get the money back to you, Mom – whenever ya' need it." Toot was pulling through a duffle, checking for his stuff.

"It's alright. It's paid for. Just keep it." Toot's Mother was clear - she had strength in the set of her jaw. "I wish I knew - what it's all about."

"Me too," Toot looked happy, "and when I do, you'll be the first to hear about it, Mom."

"On the six o'clock news, I bet."

They smiled at each other; it was the same sort of smile.

Then Toot looked off towards the peninsula like a dog Jerry had once. He was edgy.

"Jerry?'

"Yeah."

"Would you take my Mother back with you in the dinghy? Keep her there for a while?"

"Oh, now, Toot. Don't bother Jer-"

"Can ya'?"

"Good idea." Jerry had a bunker - they'd be safe there.

Then Toot went inside.

Lynne Doddie

"Hey girlie girl."

Lynne felt like she was waking up from the dead. "oh gee."

"I'm getting out of town - wanna' come?"

This had to be the worst hangover she ever had. "What?"

"To where I'm going." It was the kid from the supermarket except he looked like John Garfield in *Four Daughters* - not like a kid anymore - more like a man.

"Come on. This town isn't for you and me. Come on."

Lynne wished Toullaine was here and all of a sudden she felt *real bad*. Like out of the blue - *real bad*.

"It'll all sort out. Trust me."

He looked so honest, Lynne wanted to believe him.

The kid picked her up and carried her outside and put her in a jeep. Then he gave a woman a hug and shook Jerry's hand and then he got in behind the wheel, and they took off together leaving all that Lynne ever knew behind.

THE POOL

The Pool

It was a suburb really but due to its proximity to the foothills, it had a tucked in quality - more like a village, and the homes were of an earlier generation so that only 1 in 4 houses had identical floorplans and even then porches and side porches and the placement of the garage disguised that, so it took getting inside to know the sameness. But the same it was - that is the nature of a suburb. The houses and the people and the maple trees had a sameness. It was a nice place to grow up in. The people there had similar values and the same color skin and the choice of the Catholic Church or the Dutch Reformed, and practically everyone made an effort to get along - no one made a fuss - even the Fall one of the Honey sisters spent 3 weeknights out of 5 drinking straight shots of vodka at the bar at the St. Rita's Inn - or the time 2 of the Riley boys dug up Judge Stone's gravestone and put it in the depot beside the pot belly stove. That was on a Halloween and everyone had been expecting something like that more or less and heaved a sigh of relief and shook their heads and smiled when that was all it was. That is what this story is about - Halloween in that suburb at that time.

The local grammar school and the newly built high school paid service to Halloween when it came on a weekday and it usually did. The grammar school had a party and a costume parade to which parents were invited after lunch, and the high school lent its auditorium to the town for the Halloween Dance. The high school students themselves were in charge of decorations and there usually was a terror tunnel made out of refrigerator and TV console boxes and a wash bucket for apple dunking and a treat table provided by the PTA. It was a nice place to grow up in.

Set back from the town on a rise in one of the foothills, there was a one story house made of fieldstone with light blue trim and beveled glass windows that divided interior light into its many diamond shaped panes and even at night kept curious eyes out. It was impossible to see in if anyone dared to step up to one of those windows which certainly no adult did and children usually avoided except of course on Halloween. This is a story about Halloween. This is a story about sameness.

The fieldstone house was nestled close to the ground in a wood of white birches. There was a steep hill that rolled down from the house and ended in a pool. The pool was fed by a stream that ran down the foothills and across the yard and was dammed at the far end by a man-made fieldstone wall that slowed down the stream and made a pool with a waterfall at the far end. On still days, the pool reflected the sky and the house perfectly. On windy days, it was dark.

In the house lived a blond woman-girl of exquisite beauty. No one had ever seen her close up or at least no one ever claimed to have seen her up close, but at twilight, wives and mothers and sometimes fathers and children had seen her following through the birches in the yard or sometimes standing utterly still and appearing as a figure in a painting of the fieldstone house and yard - a provocative presence - Wyeth like - who encouraged wonder and speculation but very little - for a small town - talk. She usually wore white with a touch of blue and the material was such that it flowed with her like the softest breeze - her dress was a caress to her beauty. She was petit. Even from that distance, it was clear she was petit. There was a symmetry to the way she held her arms, her hands, her head, and when she moved, it was effortless, and her blond hair shone like a halo. There seemed to be about her felicity. She was attractive and yet people kept their distance.

No one in town spoke of knowing her or of speaking to her or of calling her up and asking her to join in town functions. None of the men in town except for Joe Poole had any dealings with her and Joe received payment for lawn maintenance and general handiwork around the house - exterior only - through the mail. Someone once asked Joe how he got that job but all he said was his family had always done it - his father had done it - and his father before him - and they didn't have any dealings with the owners. The house itself had been there certainly before the suburbs and was probably as old as the town and for the children of the town took its place in haunted house lore since they had no other in this tidy suburb where the only empty houses were company owned and usually didn't stay empty long enough to gain attention.

On Goosey Night, which was in those parts the name for the night before Halloween but known as Mischief Night in other towns, the children of the town had rituals to attend to that included: standing under the railroad trestle in the dark; scaring each other in the graveyard; toilet papering bushes and trees; ringing doorbells and running away; soaping windows, and letting the air out of bike tires if anybody in town was fool enough to leave theirs out. Halloween itself began after lunch with the costume parade and contest in school followed by trick or treating the whole town if a child had the determination and time in the 3 hours left before dinner. The trick or treating traditionally started with penny candy left out by old man Nickleman on the front step of Nickleman's Candy & Tobacco Store. All the children in that town did all these things every Goosey Night and Halloween - not at the same time - not all in large groups - but all the children did it. All the children also went out of their way to pass by the fieldstone house with the pale blue trim and at least have a look for on Halloween night, the house and the yard and the woods in back too were decorated.

There were beaten metal satin-black cats with their backs arched and shocked at intervals all the way up the half semi-circle that was the quarter mile path to the front door. There were beautifully cast ceramic pumpkins with orange glaze lit up yellow across the rain gutter on the roof. There were azure blue and pale green lights behind each pane of beveled glass. There were tiny silken witches with long white hair on broomsticks floating in the breeze from the birches. There were miniature cloth cornstalks arranged in likely formation on the side of the hill that led down to the pool. And in the pool on little barges were flames of fire delicately licking the dark above and catching floating fragments - dabs really - of the house itself in the dark below. Finally, hanging from the grape arbor that trellised a portion of the path were wind chimes that filled the yard with fluttering tinkles and pings and pongs and pangs.

Joe Poole did it. He found an envelope with his name on it on the shed door every Goosey Night. Inside the envelope on pale blue stationery were beautifully handwritten instructions and a map of the yard indicating the precise placement of each ornament and effect. A postscript always followed the instructions suggesting that when he finished, he slip the envelope and its contents under the back door, which he did. Inside the shed were ornaments gleaming from every nook, cranny, workbench and box. Joe Poole took them out and did as he was instructed then returned them to the shed so by All Saints Day, which was the day after Halloween, they were gone.

One year while he was taking the ceramic pumpkins off the roof, one dropped and broke into a hundred twinkling pieces at his feet and he felt more than saw her presence so that when he went to drop the fragments into the trash, he though better of it and slipped the pieces into a manila envelope and left it on the back porch leaning up against the back door with the word *sorry* scrawled in his gruff hand on the flap, and in the morning, it was gone.

Joe Poole was a married man with five daughters and one son but Joe Poole in that private recess, which is the soul's, knew that he loved the exquisite girl-woman whose property he maintained.

He couldn't remember not loving her though he hadn't taken over from his Dad until he was a full 18 and although he knew of her - town lore - he'd only let her into the corner of his eye before that, and hadn't felt her presence fully until he'd cut her lawn. It was odd that he and his father and his Grandfather never had discussed the girl-woman or her ancestors but they never did.

So every Halloween, the town came out and looked at the house and yard, and clusters of housewives would *ooh* and *aah* and occasionally lightly applaud the beauty in the yard, but no one except the odd newcomer - usually a child - ever approached the front door. One year a mistaken boy not more than 6 years of age who was visiting a family on Oak Terrace for Halloween went all the way up the path through the grape arbor and all the cats, and knocked on the door. When no one answered, he knocked again and again and when still no one came, he walked back down the path and went on to the next house. That was what happened. No one answered the door when somebody came even the odd salesman or the gas man who was new and didn't know the territory. No one in the fieldstone house with the pale blue trim answered the door, not even on Halloween.

For her part, the exquisite girl-woman seemed to enjoy her twilights in her yard. In the Winter when the storms came, she'd be bundled up in a long and perfectly tailored sheepskin overcoat with her tiny feet laced in genuine mukluks. Sometimes people saw her from their windows or from their cars peruse the hidden shapes that grew in her garden. Joe Poole climbed her deeply pitched roof at regular intervals and loosened melting snow so no glissade - however tiny - let loose as she walked by. In the Spring, she seemed to admire the multi-colored tulips that flooded her gardens and the daffodils that sprung up like surprise on the hillside by the pool. Joe Poole dug up the bulbs and replanted them faithfully each year ensuring full blooms. In the Summer, she'd stop by the yellow roses that grew to perfect height and stem strength along the southern wall of the house; she'd lean over and take a long and enduring whiff; their fragrance was subtle but seemed to stun her delicate sense of smell. When these overreached their bloom, Joe Poole snipped off the offending buds so no rose ever showed up wilt. In the Fall, she watched the yellow flutter of her birches and the crisp oranges of her oaks that stood up straight and capped the woods but she watched this feast from inside from an open window at the front or the back of the house. Indeed, people in the town when they saw her in the Fall, if they saw her at all, only caught her glimpsing from one window or another and at that she'd only stay framed for as long as it took to see the changing scene, then the hinged and beveled glass would shut firmly against the Fall.

No one knew why the girl-woman didn't venture into twilight in the Fall though there were those who speculated she suffered asthma and others who claimed she went abroad in September; the truth was her exquisite beauty could not bear the slow dance of death that Fall brought to her yard. Perhaps that was why she decorated on Halloween - to celebrate Fall's passing and a new beginning in the sleep of Winter's earth, for on no other holiday - or for no other season - did she have Joe Poole decorate her yard.

The contractor's wife was a buxom woman who wore floral dresses and carried a navy blue handbag and drove a dark green Buick. It was a special color ordered just for her from the local auto dealership out on Route 23. Other that that, the contractor's wife seemed like a perfectly normal housewife who ran the Hospital Volunteer Association with an iron fist, and went to services on Sunday at the Dutch Reformed Church, and minded other people's business when it suited her or her husband.

The contractor's wife's husband's family had lived in town for generations - probably since the town became a township back in 1701. The town was old. The contractor's family affiliation with the town was old. The fieldstone house with the pale blue trim was older. This was why the foothills with its encompassing meadows, lakes and streams belonged to the fieldstone house with the pale blue trim and not to the contractor's family, and this was why the trouble began.

111

It was a Saturday in September - Indian Summer was outside - and the volunteers of the Hospital Volunteer Association were pulling into the asphalt parking lot that ran alongside the chain linked yard that held the contractor's heavy equipment like tractors and steam rollers and shovels and rams. Most of the volunteers had new model cars - this year's or last's - so the parking lot looked like a new car lot at sunset - fenders had gloss and grillwork sparkled. Most of the husbands in town went over to the firehouse on Saturdays and let the Boy Scouts wash their automobiles - 25 cents for interiors. It was a good opportunity to kid around and it kept the youngsters busy.

There were gathering clouds in the blues and grays and pinks of that September sky that contrasted to the warmth in the air enough so that several volunteers were standing looking up when the contractor's wife arrived. The contractor's wife had a mission that night so the sooner she gathered her flock into the offices in the warehouse that were her husband's the better. She waved a tightfisted, gloved hand to the stragglers and hoped they'd take the hint. She hated meetings that ran late. That was why she always got there exactly on time and strode quickly to the front of whichever room it was and started or hoped for the start of any meeting she attended. Some people in town joked they could set their watches to the minute by her comings and goings, and she didn't mind the teasing as long as they were on time.

That night at the dinner table, the contractor hadn't been able to eat. He'd pushed his mashed potatoes around on his plate and squished his peas like a brat. So she'd excused their 3 children (just about every family in town had 3 children) from kitchen cleanup to the TV and poured herself and him two clean cups of freshly percolated coffee. She also turned off the chandelier over the table in favor of the less illuminating corner lamp.

The contractor got right to the point. He knew she didn't like to beat around the bush. He'd been a good husband in that respect - he considered her time. What it boiled down to was: the contractor had overextended himself on a job for a nearby township - although everybody had assured him it was a simple matter of incorporation - that it was simply a matter of time - and like a fool, he'd believed them - and now there was a question about the actual town limits for crying out loud - and the township's standing with the state depended on a completely new survey that could take months - and the road system they'd ordered was already laid and paved - the contractor had held up his end of the deal - and they couldn't collect the property taxes they needed to pay him until the survey established the taxpayers and on top of everything else, it was just possible half the road system would fall outside town limits and if that happened - the contractor was finished - just finished - and the whole thing could take months - a year even - and the contractor didn't have a year!!

When he started pacing up and down in front of the picture window, the contractor's wife shut the blinds. When he raised his voice and yelled bankruptcy, she shut the doors. When he broke down crying on her new ottoman, she shut herself inside her mind and clicked away the possibilities.

That night she told the hospital volunteers they'd raised enough for the new pediatric wing of the hospital. She reminded everybody this fund-raiser had been generously gotten off the ground with a $5000 check donated by the AT&T family who'd subsequently moved out of town after their 11 year old son had been struck with polio probably from swimming in the sandpit which all the children in town had been explicitly told not to do. The contractor's wife was relieved to report the boy had survived and was doing well as could be expected in Utah and that the AT&T family was not after all insisting that the new pediatric wing be named after their boy. And so after two years and two months of phone calls and bake sales and countless card parties and fashion shows, they'd reached their goal.

The lie didn't stick in her throat; it lodged there and waited. The room was still and disbelieving. Then her officers stood up one by one and clapped their hands. True - they'd been taken unawares but they were determined to show support even though she had agreed to hold off on this until at least the annual Christmas Bazaar. And so what if they weren't precisely at goal - she must know what she was doing. The contractor's wife waited for the ripple of applause to make its way around the room and was irritated to see a hand go up towards the back.

It was one of the executives from the pharmaceutical plant out on Route 23. He and his family were fairly new in town so the contractor's wife wasn't all that sure what he had to say. Well - he had plenty to say: The bedrock foundation upon which the hospital had been built wasn't bedrock at all but shale which was fine for cornfields but far too close to the river to guarantee the foundations for more that 50 to 60 years and maybe that was fine for now - spilt milk and all - but the planning board wasn't likely to make the same mistake twice.

After another moment of stunned silence, everybody had something to say including the contractor's wife who rapped the room into attention. She was determined to win whatever debate cropped up but to do it, order was needed. The contractor's wife didn't like the executive from the pharmaceutical plant. He knew too much for a newcomer. Shale, indeed.

Joe Poole was digging up daffodil bulbs and tossing them into an old bushel basket he had when the contractor's wife and several of the gals from the Hospital Volunteer Association came gabbing up the quarter mile turn to the fieldstone house. They'd come out of nowhere leaving Joe without the time to retreat to the toolshed. He wasn't much of a talker - Joe Poole - neither was his wife. They were both too darn tired at the end of the day to discuss much of anything and that left Joe short on small talk so he hoped like sixty the contractor's wife and her cronies hadn't come to see him - except of course, they had. The contractor's wife was waving from the path – afraid, he supposed, to step on the velvet seagreen lawn that had been cultivated for the last 6 generations by Joe and the men in his family.

Joe took his time slapping the reddish sod from his khakis and rubbing his hands together before he climbed the hill to the constituency. The contractor's wife went first.

Joe Poole thought it was good they'd found out about the shale. For the past 300 years, his family had lived on the land down by the river and worked it and Joe could remember his Father's disquietude and then honest surprise when the planning board had acquisitioned a parcel of their land for less than the going rate for the then new hospital. There was shale all over their land - anybody knew that - but folks like Joe Poole and his Father didn't tell folks like the contractor and his wife what was what. They'd let the planning board have their way and had given up 6 acres of bottom land without much fuss, so if anything Joe was glad that in the ensuing 30 years they'd discovered the shale and wouldn't be bothering him or his sisters for another parcel.

She was in the window at the far corner of the house - the girl-woman was there - like a soft flame. Joe Poole felt her eyes in his. The contractor's wife caught the glow in Joe's eyes and turned to look but the beveled window clicked shut and filled its diamond shapes with reflections.

Joe Poole told the volunteers that he didn't know but if he had to guess, he supposed that the woman here on this land wouldn't sell off acreage for the new hospital. The contractor's wife explained it was for the good of the town - she didn't mention her husband. Joe Poole said folks didn't like their land getting yanked which was a strong thing for a man like Joe Poole to say. The contractor's wife said she'd see about that and took the rest of the path in stride all the way up to the front door. The others gals followed along excited-like - too curious to be afraid. Joe Poole stayed where he was.

The contractor's wife knocked on the door then folded her hands down in front of her and waited. No one answered. The contractor's wife knocked on the door again - this time using the knocker made of brass. It sounded in the neighborhood 3 times and a dog barked two streets over in response. The volunteers re-shuffled themselves on the path. But still no one answered. She banged again - this time with force and repetition. The sound of it echoed off the foothills and some of the crows in the oaks behind the house began to make a fuss. 10 times, 11 times, 15 times. Some of the volunteers were getting uncomfortable. The contractor's wife was red-faced and sweating. It wasn't like her. They started back down the path in fits and starts - a straggly line - some of them afraid to stay - more of them afraid to go.

Joe Poole stood there and watched. There was nothing he could do. If the contractor's wife wanted to bang on the door, there was nothing he could do to stop her. Besides he was curious to see if the inhabitor would come to the door though he knew in his heart, she would not.

The contractor's wife stopped banging on the door. She had a hot, stale feeling in her mouth. The silence that ensued was full. It beat in her ears like rain. She turned and faced the volunteers. If she wasn't cautious, she'd lose control and the contractor's wife couldn't lose control. Two of them twitched her a nervous smile.

Joe Poole watched the parade of hospital volunteers follow the contractor's wife back down the path and through the grape arbor. When they passed by him, he stepped aside and didn't mind that only two of them gave him a nod. It was war. Joe Poole wondered who would win.

There was a peace in the valley but not the peace of many seasons filling the air with its reflected glow like trees who stand and wait a hundred years, their limbs tossed confidently at a sky that lets them grow so the trees in exchange seem to fill a space greater than their own and spray the sky with a tessellated sort of nimbus. This peace belonged before a storm.

The contractor had 2 new Selectric IBM typewriters and his own personal electronic calculator removed from his office at the warehouse and installed in the breakfast nook of his wife's kitchen. The contractor considered it smart to separate the business from his wife's force although at no other time in their 23 year old marriage had they been more partners. She would do her part to secure the land - he would secure the bid on the new hospital.

The IBM's clicked and typed up what the contractor's wife commanded. The hospital volunteers arrived in twos in 2 hour intervals throughout the days and carried in and out her orders. The contractor's wife had an iron touch with people. She succeeded in intimidating them but never to the point they stayed away. She created a magnetic field of communal good deeds that inspired respect if not affection, and through the years steamrolled this effect into an unimpeachable record of getting the job done.

She should have been in politics and might well have been a Nixon-sort of candidate had she not been born both rigid and female. Female politicians had a pretty sort of backyard gentleness - well-spoken, well-bobbed - that said they had a recipe or two up their sleeves. The contractor's wife had none of these. She was a hard worker, resourceful up to a point, with no particular charm. 23 years earlier, the contractor's Mother had insisted upon a traditional wedding in the Dutch Reformed Church so the contractor's then fiancée had walked down the aisle alone (no amount of cajoling changed that) in a huge white dress of tulle and lace looking for all the world like a snowbank. That was the last time the contractor's wife had listened to anything but her own council.

There were letters to be drafted to the town council as well as the planning board as well as every registered voter in the community. That meant there were a lot of envelopes that had to be hand-written since the mailing labels on file excluded folks like Joe Poole and his family unless they happened to be members of the Volunteer Fire Association. It was unlikely they belonged to The Rotary Club or The Elks and they wouldn't be on the registry of the Dutch Reformed Church since Joe Poole and folks like him usually belonged to the Catholic Church and the only Catholics on the contractor's mailing list were police. It was just a matter of business and there wasn't any point in permanently entering their addresses.

The contractor's wife thought long and hard about that first letter - the one to the town. She didn't want to alienate anybody. She praised the Hospital Volunteers for their effort and mentioned the beautiful location at the foot of the hills the Planning Board had selected. She pointed out that the Town Council was aware the location might inconvenience some of the families who lived along the south side of Mountain Avenue for 6 months to a year but that in the long run, they'd have a new hospital at their doorsteps and freshly landscaped lawns and shrubs right across the road. She didn't say anything about parking lots or the First Aid Squad or the housing for the hospital generators or the possibility that in the next 10 years, the planning board might decide to put up another firehouse at the same location. There weren't enough votes on Mountain Avenue to raise much of a fuss. They all had 2 acre lots and houses that cost too much in the first place. In the last paragraph, she mentioned that she was hopeful the single occupant on the north side of Mountain Avenue would be cooperative in the Township's efforts.

The letter laid the seed. It was the town council and the planning board and the hospital volunteers against the single occupant on the north side of Mountain Avenue. If push came to shove, and the contractor's wife loved a fight, other carefully worded letters would build her case until the whole town was up in arms.

The Landmark Committee expressed the concern that although the owner had never requested it and the committee had never so designated it, the fieldstone house with the pale blue trim was the oldest known premises in town and it seemed a shame. The contractor's wife argued that the homes along the Boulevard were stately and designated and enough to secure the township's past without the premises on the north side of Mountain Avenue bringing a halt to its future. The Landmark Committee conferred and concurred. One of the members of the town council who happened to reside on the south side of Mountain Avenue expressed a discreet objection to the contractor himself but the contractor assured the member that a deal could be struck on a brand new home situated up in the foothills - *what a view* - once that land was freed up. There was one other objection raised.

Joe Poole parked his pickup in front of the contractor's house on a Tuesday night and walked up the white gravel driveway and hand-delivered a pale blue envelope to the contractor's wife. The contractor's wife took it and after a terse *thank-you* stared at Joe. She had no intention of opening it in front of him after the surly treatment he'd handed her on the front walk to the fieldstone house. For his part, Joe was tempted to wait her out. He had no idea what was in the envelope - he only knew he'd found it on his workbench in the toolshed that Tuesday morning. In the end, Joe turned away figuring he'd find out soon enough.

The contractor's wife couldn't wait even to close the door. She stood in the shadow of the screen and ran a pudgy index finger under the lightly glued flap and pulled out a single sheet of pale blue stationary. It was folded once. She flipped it open. On it in a delicate hand was a single word: *No.*

The contractor's wife smiled. She knew just where to put it. The single sheet of blue stationary was pressed neatly by itself behind the locked glass that encased announcements on the signboard outside the Dutch Reformed Church. The minister believed in the separation of church and state but *afterall* this was a good cause and what was best for the majority of his congregation. So the pale blue sheet of paper with the single word *No* became a beacon of arrogance right smack dab in the center of town.

It didn't take more. The Town Council and the Planning Board and the Hospital Volunteer Association went to work. Stronger letters went out. Special town meetings were scheduled and held. True to the inertia of the times, the first two were sparsely attended but then word of mouth saturated and because of the resulting numbers, the next 3 meetings had to be moved to the high school auditorium. The Landmark Committee organized the petition that demanded the owner of the fieldstone house enter into negotiations with the Town Council. Everyone signed – everyone, that is - but Joe Poole and folks like Joe Poole who figured one hospital was good enough for now and the foothills were kind of nice as is. Of course folks like Joe Poole had a *let-it-be* attitude that came out of hard work and figured not signing the petition was about as much as they could do.

Joe Poole's wife and the contractor's wife had gone to the same high school - the regional one at the county seat. They weren't friends there and they weren't friends here, but like all relationships that come young, they held each other in a sort of trust. The contractor's wife had seen the look in Joe Poole's eyes on the front walk to the fieldstone house that day. It was a look she'd seen before - usually glimpsed - always from a distance - never directed at her - in a man's eyes. She needed this alliance - this inroad to the townies as Joe Poole and people like him were called by people like her. She'd considered saying what she saw in Joe's eyes right out to one of the hospital volunteers; it was good enough for gossip. But some of the volunteers had seen her panic when she banged on the blue door and such a seed as this coming from her lips might set them wondering at her reason. They couldn't see her need. They could only see her concern for the community. Nobody could know the contractor's predicament. She'd have to be cautious. Her fabric would tolerate no holes. What was needed was a solid front.

Joe Poole's wife looked up.

"I need wood chopped. A parcel of wood. We're taking down the cherry trees on the back of our property. Your boy interested?"

Joe Poole's wife thought - *yes*. Her boy - her first born - was 16 soon to be 17 - and a man, and Joe Poole's wife wanted her son out of town for life. She'd never said the words not even to her sisters but she'd thought it in her mind: When Joe went to work for the fieldstone house - oh not right off - but as the summers slipped away, Joe changed in the way he was. Her son would soon take over his Father's work on the land around the fieldstone house and though that would set Joe free, Joe Poole's wife loved his son more. And so it was understood - on some primeval level - a deal was struck: Joe Poole's son would work the contractor's land.

The petition was nailed to the blue door by the reluctant chief of police and one of his men on a Friday night in early October after a pitcherfull of beer at the St. Rita's Inn. It was so loud everyone in town heard the echo of the steel-headed hammer driving the nail. The mayor's wife said later they might have used staples instead of all that racket but the contractor's wife was pleased. It suited her to draw attention to the blue door and it did draw a line of cars on weekends. Chevys and Plymouths and Fords drove slowly past as if in funeral procession and the people in the cars wondered out loud if the inhabitant had read the petition. Some thought she had - some thought no. The wife of the town council member who lived across the road said the blue door had remained shut and the recent rain had dissolved the yellow petition.

Joe Poole for his part left the nail in the blue door. He'd already found the excuse of laying a fieldstone wall along the back to check water runoff and support the hill to keep him on her land longer each day and that made good sense - he felt the obligation; but taking the nail out of the door meant trouble and Joe Poole never bought trouble.

It was late - he'd missed supper - lost in the work of the fieldstone wall - and the light bulb that hung down in the toolshed was out. He cursed it softly and shuffled blindly in the dark towards the workbench and then, like a cobweb, she was there and her breath came in a zephyr while the door to the shed banged hard once on its hinges.

Outside the dark was quiet. There was nothing in the breeze.

Men felt the difference when they got out of their cars downtown for a quart of milk or a quart of beer or the late edition. It was subdued out in that late October night - it was tame.

Joe's knees buckled as the lightbulb popped on. He smelled her in his nose like salt. He stood alone in the shed. She was gone. Outside a lonely crow cawed. A pale blue envelope was propped against a jar of nails in front of him on the shelf. He opened it and written on pale blue note paper were his instructions.

Joe was to drive to the old ferry landing in Hoboken that same Tuesday night. There he was to meet a man. The man's name was Ben Quick. Joe Poole was to tell Ben Quick all that had happened, and when he was through, he was to say these 11 words without hesitation - without the slightest pause:

violet calls the terms of the agreement now she has come

Judge Stone - not the original Oliver Prince Stone but his grandson, Judge Walter Stone - was in his offices late for a Tuesday night. It was brisk out. A wind had stirred up. Fall was in the trees. He felt safe and comfortable behind the curve of his mahogany desk entrenched in writs and wills. That's what Judge Stone did nowadays mostly - wills - as if there really were some control beyond the grave. He was getting on and so were his clients - folks in town who remembered it as the farming community it had been when Judge Stone was a boy and not the sprawling suburb it was quickly becoming - not that Judge Stone minded change - change was good for business. A scratching came at the window. He thought it was a bush. It turned out to be the hospital volunteers.

Three of them - the 3 main ones Judge Stone guessed - stood on the other side of his desk - they wouldn't sit down - the fat one was the contractor's wife. What they wanted was a way to turn the woman on the north side of Mountain Avenue off her land. Judge Stone knew all about the plans for the new hospital. He also knew that all the land on the north side of Mountain Avenue which included the foothills had been granted by one of the Kings of England - he wasn't positive which one - and that in the year 1748, the township itself had agreed to tax immunity for all the land north of Mountain Avenue in exchange for all the land south of Mountain Avenue, not including the tract held by the Poole family that ran along the river. He didn't point this out to the hospital volunteers. He wasn't sure which side of the political fence he was on yet. He could argue it either way. The fat one was saying there had to be something they could do, and since the original land grant had been made in pre-Revolutionary times, Judge Stone knew that there was. What he told the hospital volunteers that night was that he'd take a look into it.

Joe Poole arrived at the old ferry dock in Hoboken at the exact same time the contractor's wife scratched at Judge Stone's window. It was deserted. The dock itself had fallen to disrepair. Joe sat in his pickup and wondered when the last ferry would run out of here. It wasn't a practical operation anymore - with the tunnels and the bridge. The men in town who left each morning and came back at night traveled in car pools. Joe could almost see the last ferry running out into the fog; he could almost hear its foghorn - not that he'd spent much time in Hoboken. He pulled down out of the cab and smelled the salt air running up and down the Hudson. It was good. Out on the dock 20 to 25 feet was a shed and over the shed was a sign. It was lit up in yellow. Joe walked toward it with nothing in mind. He had the idea he was watching himself walk along a dock in the middle of the night in Hoboken. A seagull screeched down and flew back out over the river. Joe looked up. The sign read **TIRES** - then underneath in small black letters **proprietor - Ben Quick.** Joe rapped on the door to the shed. There was no answer. Joe rapped again. The window to the right of the door flapped up.

"What."

"Ben Quick?"

"Yeah."

*He had the idea he was watching himself walk along
a dock in the middle of the night in Hoboken.*

"I'm Joe Poole."

And Joe told his story. At first he tried to make out the eyes but the brim of Ben Quick's hat kept moving like he was looking out for something - that and his height versus Joe's - Ben Quick was short - real short. Joe was pretty sure he was standing on a crate to come up that high at the window. And he was colored or dark-skinned at any rate. When Joe got done telling Ben Quick what was going on in town, he offered the blue note.

"Say it."

Then when Joe hesitated, "Say it. Say the words," said Ben Quick.

And Joe did:

"Violet calls the terms of the agreement she has come."

There is a space in time for change open like a vacuum empty. It is unseen but there. It lies still in the planes and shafts of daylight, in the darker darks of night. It does not roam or climb or search. Like a dormant ballfield, it waits for human frailty.

Joe Poole's wife rode over to the contractor's that Wednesday before Halloween with her big boy up front. He was uneasy about clearing the contractor's land, she knew, but he wanted to be a man. Usually he rode in back on the flatbed of the pickup standing up holding on if she didn't stop him but now he rode up front. He wanted to be a man.

Joe Poole's son felt eager and anxious. Clearing woods was fit for him but killing trees struck deep in Pooles. All he'd ever had at was a big old stump his Father put him on in front of town hall. It had taken him a whole day of sweating to pull those roots free. He swallowed hard.

Joe Poole's wife watched her son's Adam apple roll over in his throat. He hadn't told his Dad about the job. Some instinct held him back she guessed. She was glad. She didn't want *no words* with Joe. Joe was a steady man. If trouble came out of this, she'd bear it. She downshifted and turned in on the drive.

The contractor's wife stood in the middle.

Joe Poole's son watched her coming at him in the windshield. There was a breeze lickin' at her skirt made the muscles of her thighs stick out and her hair was loose and singing in the breeze and her eyes shone dark like coals. He pulled his eyes out of hers and looked across for his Mom but she was down already out of the cab waiting with the contractor's wife for him to do the same.

He followed them around back. The contractor's wife showed him where she wanted the cherry wood stacked; she said she'd burn it this winter and *won't that be a sweet smell*. Joe Poole's son felt a trickle of sweat on the back of his neck. He slapped at it - *darn*. Then he followed her out across the lawn. They had gophers - early signs - he wanted to say so, show what he knew but a look from his Mom held his tongue still.

The contractor's wife was turned at the gate saying something and he watched her jacket fall open and the big pink flowers in her dress pull tight on her tits. *What in hell* was wrong with him? The contractor's wife was a dog - well, not a dog maybe - but old. Joe Poole's son was sweating bullets now. He sure hoped the contractor's wife couldn't see what he was feeling or he'd never get the job.

His Mom was leaving.

"Mom?," his voice croaked.

His Mother turned back and looked at her big boy.

The contractor's wife held herself still on the far side of the fence.

He looked like a boy - just a boy - *her boy*. Joe Poole's wife felt something like fear creep up on her. Was she doing right?

The breeze picked up and the orchard moved.

"You'll get home on your own then," was what Joe Poole's wife heard herself say.

Joe Poole's son watched his Mom go then he turned back. The contractor's wife was deep in the orchard. He followed her in.

"These trees here - they're fine." He was saying it like he'd heard his Dad saying it a hundred times - exact.

The contractor's wife was pulling at some dead wood.

"Here, lemme'." He grabbed on.

This cherry orchard was fine too. The limbs on the trees were hard and smooth like steel. He could hear them standing still. The cracked limb pulled off.

The contractor's wife felt flushed. She didn't like it in here with all these trees.

"Now them over there - they got rot. I could clean 'em out for you." He felt surer now.

The contractor's wife pulled at her jacket. She felt hot. She pulled it off.

On the outer rim, it was true; it was time to plant new. He wanted to tell her what he knew - he felt like he'd feel good if he told her - if he told her about the English Morellos out at the nursery on Route 23 but all he could think was how her nipples were growing like cherry pits in the skin of her pink dress.

"I want 'em all down. I want this orchard down," she said.

The trees grew up around him; he could feel them reaching in the wind.

"Yeah, but ma'am..."

She took a step nearer.

The orchard groaned.

"I want 'em down."

Joe Poole's son felt the arm of a cherry limb press hard in the small of his back.

She felt wild like a storm - and wet.

The breeze picked up and the orchard moved.

He couldn't take his eyes *offa'* her - she looked just like Anna Magnani looked in *The Fugitive Kind.*

She felt vulnerable and confused - she took a misstep back. And he caught her by the arm.

And she saw what he was seeing in his eyes and she felt new - for the first time in her life - new.

He wanted to say something but he couldn't get the words to come clean.

And she felt powerful too - all that young boy's power coming into her and it wasn't the struggle each step of her life had been. It was just standing there - waiting there - like it'd always been there waiting just for her. The contractor's wife reached.

In the valley, there was a belling. There was a keening. There was a wordless cry. It came from in the fieldstone house and rendered the air hollow. There was catalepsy on the fields. No creature moved or uttered. There was no bleat or mew. Infelicity roared and ran across the foothills like a shadow and no one in town heard it for what it was except the dogs and trees.

"What was that?" The mayor's wife was at the window.

Two women looked over. "Sounds like a gull," one of them said.

"This far in? No. A seagull? Not here," murmured through the room.

The hospital volunteers were in the church house fixing candles to cardboard holders constructed and colored by the students of the 1st and 2nd grades. The whole town was hard at work on the candlelit procession set for 7:00 P.M. that very night out on Mountain Avenue. It was no coincidence it was Goosey night. The hospital volunteers figured on the activity keeping all the kids in town busy and out of trouble too. Nobody was at home this afternoon. Most businesses had agreed to close early - about 3:00 P.M.

The mayor's wife watched a seagull land on the signboard outside the Church. It was unusual - a seagull this far inland.

The Secretary of the Landmark Committee came in vexed from across the hall. She needed to speak with the contractor's wife. The mayor's wife said she was in temporary charge. And what was it? Well - it seemed the Boy Scouts of America were here to collect the posters - the ones with the hundred ice blue flames representing saved lives, overlaid by the blood red cross representing the new hospital and nobody could find them. Where were they? The Secretary then took the time to remind the hospital volunteers that the posters had been designed by the ad-executive husband of the President of the Landmark Committee. It was generally known that the President herself and the contractor's wife had been in some disagreement over the date of distribution - the contractor's wife seeing it as a final blitzkrieg effort and the President of the Landmark Committee viewing it as more of a first attack. One of the wryer hospital volunteers said in lieu of their disappearance perhaps this was to be a sneak attack. Several women chuckled.

That's when 3 members of the Ladies' Society peeked in from upstairs where they were telephoning the roll of registered voters unaccounted for by the various organizations supporting the cause. They asked what the trouble was though they already knew. In the retelling, the Secretary of the Landmark committee became quite rattled. She just wanted everybody to know that her President was just across the hall *just fit to be tied*, and as far as the Landmark Committee was concerned - *that was that* for them - meaning if the posters didn't show up, they would never again support the contractor's wife or any of her dealings with the hospital volunteers!

The black wall phone in the contractor's kitchen rang and rang. The turquoise princess phone in the contractor's bedroom rang and rang. Nobody in the contractor's house answered the phones and nobody in the church house found the posters.

Judge Walter Stone was up to his knees in old case studies - histories of the town - local ordinances - that sort of thing - when he found it. It was only a paragraph, not much more than a clause in a larger body of township law set down in the Spring of 1781, pre-dating the state constitution but rendering null and void any agreement held with the kings of England. Judge Stone smacked his lips. It said right here under his nose that any tract of land heretofore uncultivated and not for the common good that fell within township limits could be acquired by filing a record and living on and cultivating said tract or any section therein contained. It went on to specify 10 acre lots...*uh-huh*...there was a requirement for split rail fencing along all boundaries...*uh-huh*. Judge Stone got up out of his leather chair and did a jig on the Persian rug right there in his office. God bless the Garden State. God bless the agricultural roots of these United States. Uncultivated - now there was a word a litigator could hang a deposition on - *yessir*. All the land on the north side of Mountain Avenue with the exception of the acre or so around the fieldstone house was to Judge Stone's certain knowledge - **uncultivated.**

His aging secretary was at the open door to his inner office with the Knights of Columbus. How long had they been standing there? Had she buzzed - *confound it?* Judge Stone pulled an extended fist out of the air above his head, set his foot back down, shook their hands 1 - 2 and offered them a seat and coffee. The Knights of Columbus took the seats, refused the coffee, and asked the Judge about his good spirits.

Whenever the Judge didn't want to divulge information, he relied on his twinkle - as his wife put it. With all seriousness, he said he'd just found a way around the Sunday blue laws and was organizing every able-bodied man in town to stampede the St. Rita's Inn this very Sunday A.M.

That got them - once they realized he was joking. Judge Stone sat down behind his desk and watched the Knights of Columbus laugh. This could be a tricky meeting. He needed these men on his side. Without them, no politician in the county - whole state for that matter - could get re-elected and Judge Stone wanted another term. Their ranks would build the new hospital, creating jobs for their unions but so far they'd been edgy about developing the land on the north side of Mountain Avenue. Judge Stone figured the best he could do was let them talk.

After a perfunctory nod towards good cause and all, the Knights expressed their doubts about future construction on their home turf. This was *afterall* their home town - they didn't want a city. Their parents had moved out of overcrowded tenements to give them fresh air and they wanted the same for their kids.

Judge Stone nodded. It was true. The land that was the town proper was used up by 50 foot lots and 2 story houses and gravel driveways and car ports and fire hydrants and cement sidewalks and lilac bushes and forsythia clipped back. Pruned maple trees lined up on every street including Elm Street. Parking meters stood in the municipal parking lot instead of the wood of swamp berry and birch that had been there just 10 years ago. Judge Stone's eyes came to rest on the vacant lot that was diagonally across the street from his offices on the corner of Post Road. It was the last vacant lot in town - held up in the old Post estate - prime.

The Knights were talking about the new shopping center on the old town green. Judge Stone himself had balked at that one but he had to admit it was convenient having a 5&Dime down the street and his wife liked the new beauty parlor. One of the Knights - the one who had served in Korea - was pointing out that the town green had been the last real stretch of open land except for the acreage on the north side of Mountain Avenue.

Judge Stone nodded. There was something itching these boys that went beyond good cause and fresh air and that was this: Some in town had more; some in town had less; but everybody in town had more or less the same - all except the woman out on the north side of Mountain Avenue. Nobody remembered it was her people made the township possible. Beyond himself and a few other old timers, Judge Stone doubted anybody knew. It served his town not to know.

They were getting down to it. The First Aid Squad needed housing for the new ambulance the township was buying and the only place left for it was the ball field behind the firehouse. The penny dropped. Judge Stone nodded. Inside he twinkled. They wanted a new playing field. The Knights of Columbus wanted a ball field. The Elks wanted a golf course; the Ladies' Society a country club with a pool. Everybody's got their price. The Knights were talking about the Little League; the Men's Softball Team had gone to the state finals last summer. Judge Stone nodded. The library and the firehouse had gone up in his Grandfather's time; the old hospital and the grammar school in his Father's. This was good - this ball field - good for the business of his town. They were talking locker rooms - Judge Stone didn't know about that - whether the town council would agree to that - *ah, what the hell - let 'em dream*. There was still plenty of room for the development of the luxury homes proposed by the contractor and set for the tops of the hills.

He stood up, shook their hands 1 - 2. They all three knew a deal had been struck. Judge Walter Stone saw the Knights of Columbus to the door, watched them get in their cars, and was positively salivating by the time he climbed down the steps to his offices for his luncheon appointment with the mayor and 2 of the fellows on the town council. He knew which side he was on now. He knew what to do with the homesteading clause he'd found in the town council minutes of 1781 - *yessir*. The demographics on this thing were just too good. He crossed the street diagonally to his car and was about to slip the key in the lock on the driver's side when something in the vacant lot on the corner of Post Road and the Boulevard caught his eye. Judge Stone came around his car and looked.

Swamp cherries slid up in the sky and formed a sort of patchwork blue and yellow with twigs and branches in-between. It reminded him of something - looking up - when he was a boy.

Kids were always doing that - looking up. There was a game they played lying on their backs looking up except now when he looked up, he got a crick in his neck. And there it was again - something in the vacant lot made him look. It could have been a seagull. Judge Stone stepped off the sidewalk. Weeds crunched underfoot. A chipmunk ran across his shoe - made him jump. Judge Stone had to laugh. It was dense in here - smell of rotting leaves - so overgrown the whole town was blocked out. He looked back out through a bush to his car. A cardinal flashed by, landed on a bare forsythia shoot and bobbed up and down. There was an old walnut tree up ahead, towards the center of the lot, had a hole in the trunk. When he got up to it, he reached in - nothing. Judge Stone felt cheated; any tree with a hole in it ought to have some sort of treasure. But then his fingers felt a metal something and he pulled it out. It was an old cracker box - the kind his Mother used to have. *how about that* Judge Stone tried to pull it open. It wouldn't give. He sat down on a fallen tree trunk and ran his ignition key in under the lid. The lid popped off. The trees around him rustled. Inside the cracker box, there was a bird's nest and a chipped mica arrowhead and a chewed wad of gum, and a bunch of stick matches. There was also a note wrapped with string around a rock. Judge Stone undid it. The note said:

Meet you there.

Walter

It took Judge Stone several seconds to recognize the boy version of his own handwriting. He was this Walter. This tin box treasure was someone's - someone he'd known as a boy. Who? Judge Stone sat there for the longest while with a deep and abiding longing for the open fields of his youth.

Telephones in town practically rang off their hooks with the news of Judge Stone's death. The body was discovered by the Doctor's son when he was finishing up his paper route on Post Road. Some were all for going ahead with the candlelit procession set for 7:00 P.M.; others felt it should be held off in deference to the family; the contractor's wife, when she finally did pick up her own phone, ended all discussion. The best way to honor Walter Stone was to press onward - to forge ahead. She told a white lie when she said she had personally been assured that the Judge's careful consideration of the matter had been in his mind resolved and that he was all for the new hospital.

Some say that evil has a color - dark. The Bible holds to this naming dark the color of Cain. A lot happened in town that Wednesday but like most things that happen, they were only noticed one by one.

Joe Poole's son sat knees up in the twilight. He was riding along in the back of his cousin's pickup drinking Budweiser beer and feeling like a man. He shut his eyes and felt the soft trickle of carbonation slide down his throat. It was good. Life was good. It was so good. The pickup jerked to a stop. Several battered half full cans of oil paint banged in over the side.

"Hey!" He stood up. "What's the idea?"

Somebody handed him a bushel basket of rotten tomatoes then two of his buddies climbed in. This would be a Goosey night like no other Goosey night and probably their last. They all knew it too.

The wives and mothers in town gathering out on Mountain Avenue felt surely the girl-woman in the fieldstone house would have to come out now. That was the least she could do - tell the township why she wouldn't sell. The men in town gathering there said it didn't matter a damn if she came out or not - either way they were getting her land. The youngsters in town there were glad to be out on a school night.

The 8 year old daughter of the Dutch Reformed minister held the county record for most Girl Scout cookies sold and wasn't afraid of the dark. Usually in a game of hide n' seek, no one could find her because she had the knack for shadows and holding still. If somebody ever asked her - say a newspaper reporter - she'd tell them that was the secret - *shadows and holding still.* The minister's daughter had an infinite imagination. She could pretend all sorts of things and hold still. She could go in her mind anywheres - say Timbuktu or Narnia or Nottingham or Heaven or even on the pitcher's mound at Yankee Stadium. That's how she came to be in the shadow of the hill by the pool on the north side of Mountain Avenue. She was holding still and nobody could find her.

The candles were damp and hard to light. Nobody knew how they'd gotten damp but it was the devil to get one to light. When somebody finally did, they all watched the wick get dimmer and dimmer until it blinked out. The 1st and 2nd graders were as disappointed as their moms; they didn't really understand what was going on but they could see like anybody that their candle holders were broke. The 2nd grade teacher, a young woman fresh out of state college, kept protesting to the parents there that she hadn't stored the candles in the dark school basement like everybody kept saying but in the 2nd grade cupboard above the sink. The Secretary of the Landmark Committee whose president could not attend for unspecified reasons said *this was a fine kettle of fish* added to the already missing posters and she'd just like to know who was running this thing.

"Start a fire." It was the contractor's wife.

Everybody turned.

Her eyes were ablaze. The contractor's wife knew sabotage when she saw it. Her eyes flicked up to a dark glazed window in the fieldstone house and for a moment - just a moment - she let herself feel pity, but it was fleeting in her heart like the beat of a clock. Many of the parents there warmed to the contractor's wife as they saw her move in their midst bringing smiles back to the disappointed faces of their 1st and 2nd grade children. The remedy was simple. They'd all of them build a big bonfire and dry out the candles and then they'd light the candles and everybody would see.

Citizens noticed the contractor's wife that night out on Mountain Avenue in a new way - she had a shine. Her hair was down and sweaty on her neck. She was chatty too. She told an ethnic joke to the volunteer firemen when they said they weren't so sure about a bonfire this late in the season. She told one about Polish people. The firemen didn't laugh. They shuffled uneasily and held their ground. It wasn't that the joke wasn't funny. It was that the contractor's wife was of Polish descent. So she told another one - this one about Italians. She told it well. She told it with relish. She watched the firemen's eyes anticipate her every word. She watched them fill up with the swell of her delivery. She watched the last grudging grin slip into place. And then she played with them - she held back - she let her lips moisten on the build. Then in that last split-second before they saw it coming, her tongue let go of the punchline and all the firemen laughed like hell.

As everybody watched but didn't really see, a midnight blueness pulled out of the dark and clung to the house and grounds like fingers from a fogbank. It reached and pulled at the lawns drawing the eyes forever up, up to the house, to the windows where the faceted diamond-shaped panes shone dark like gleam and waited for the lick of fire to come a thousand fold. It reached and pulled up drawing the eyes forever away from the pool at the foot of the hill which was by then dissolved in blue shadow.

Joe Poole stood alone in the shed of the fieldstone house. There was no light - only inky blueness sliding underneath the door. He watched it scared. Oh, he'd been scared before in the War in a foxhole with 3 dead buddies. And he'd been scared before when he was 6 after his Mom died and he woke up smelling her and so scared he told her go and then worse-scared when she never came back. Joe Poole never picked a fight; he was too big a man to pick a fight. He hadn't picked this fight either, had he? No. This wasn't his fight, was it? No. He didn't own this land. He was only the caretaker - that's all - the caretaker - Joe Poole the caretaker.

He watched the blue slide across the floor scared. He knew it for what it was scared. It touched his work boot, recessed at the contact and then like coming home climbed his legs. Joe Poole was neaped in blueness scared.

The chicken farmer was coming out along Post Road in his brand new pickup. The chicken farmer was a happy man and glad to be coming out on a frosty Wednesday night in late October to warm things up. In the back of his pickup were 3 untapped kegs of beer for the men and 2 industrial-sized coffee urns full of mulled cider and juice for the wives and kiddies - courtesy of the contractor. There had been in time many steps bringing him to this moment. In exchange for 12 chicken coops and the 3 acres of land they stood on, needed for the new sewer system, the township had met his demands for 2 new long low laying houses up-to-date and modern and an additional 50,000 hens. Out of all this came a contract arranged by the contractor and negotiated by Judge Stone with a paint manufacturer in the city for more money than the chicken farmer had ever expected to see.

Fall was in the trees and the leaves were spraying up from the pavement like deep rain puddles as he rode his truck through. That's why he said later he missed seeing the van pull out of the driveway - the leaves got in the way. They whipped across his windshield like sleet and when they cleared, the chicken farmer's brand new pickup hit the van broadside. He couldn't make out the year. He said he could recall seeing the word **TIRES** painted in big black letters coming at him in the glass.

The next thing he remembered was the smell of smoke and rotting leaves curling up his nose and Buddy Holly singing *Everyday* from way off - then the scrape of metal as somebody pulled one of the kegs across the grit on the flatbed. He called out and the grating stopped. The chicken farmer was afraid to move - afraid his neck was broke. Then the chassis lifted up like somebody or something had dropped off the back. The funny thing was the van he hit was nowheres. All that was out his windshield on Post Road were snaky piles of dead leaves in the gutters on both sides and maple trees reaching up white and clean in the nightfall.

Then he caught sight of a man in his side view mirror off the driver's side. He was walking with a lean to his left away from the chicken farmer's truck. One of the kegs was on his shoulder like it was nothing to carry. And he looked short in the reflection - real short. A wind blew up and pushed at the man. The limbs on the maple trees crackled like bones up and down the block. The man's fedora lifted up off his head and flew back at the chicken farmer's truck. The man put down the keg and ran back in the mirror towards the chicken farmer. His torso jerked when he ran - to his left. The fedora caught on the radio aerial like a Flyin-Saucer and shimmered there grey in the night. Then the chicken farmer was staring out his side window into the coal blackest face he ever did see. The whites of the eyes bulged like sap but the rest of the man's features were lost in the midnight of his face. Then a long dark hand slid out of a sleeve and reached for the chicken farmer's neck. The chicken farmer felt a dark thumb rub on his Adam's apple like luck before the dark fingers sunk into the bones at the base of his skull. The chicken farmer said there was a tingling - a sparkling up his spine - but he said this later after he'd gotten the hang of telling his story to anybody who'd listen. Mostly the chicken farmer was scared white.

"You folks - you should leave well enough alone."

It took the chicken farmer a moment to understand the dark man had spoke and by then the dark man had pulled his fedora off the radio aerial and was disappearing into the reflection in the side view mirror. The chicken farmer watched him go until he was gone. Then he sat there still as could be listening to Buddy Holly until help and the water came.

Joe Poole's wife stood at the edge of the goings-on with 2 of her sisters-in-law and watched the town scavenge for rakes and leaves. She hadn't planned on coming. Joe at dinner that night said no. His eyes caught in hers for that second when he said it.

Joe was warning her - that Joe she met in high school - that Joe that played 1st base for the other team first time she ever saw him and when he got a hit, she cried out and they all made her sit back down but he found her with his eyes and looked so sure, she knew her life would never be just hers again but hers and Joe's. She didn't know how Joe knew what she'd done. He'd just found out that's all. He had to know she had to save their son. Their boy couldn't live his life out in the service of that woman in the fieldstone house. Their son was more than that. He could be the 1st one in their families to get college. She wanted that for her 1st born bad. Joe knew it too. She'd said it all along. It was time to get up off the land. But in Joe's eyes at dinner that night was something she'd never seen before - a tiredness of the spirit that only seeks resolve.

"Joe..."

"What."

"Don't go out tonight." She just said it.

Joe had pulled down his jacket off the hook. He'd stood so still - so alone under the light by the door. Then he'd pulled it on - then his hat then his work gloves. He wouldn't give his eyes back to her, so she'd reached up and pulled on his chin and he'd bent and kissed her mouth so gentle that she cried out when he pushed into the dark through the storm door.

Joe Poole's wife felt hot regret - regret for what she'd done - regret for here and now and yesterday and all the weeks and days and minutes that took them away from each other so it seemed like now they'd never get back. It wasn't true that everything that happened was her own. It wasn't true that everything that happened was what she wanted. She wanted Joe back - back inside her dreams and hopes and not just sleeping in her bed. She wanted Joe back. Joe Poole's wife wanted Joe.

The minister's wife was saying something - *Had they seen her daughter?* Her sisters-in-law shook their heads no and they, all three, took a step back so the Minister's wife could pass.

The folks out on Mountain Avenue were getting restless. They'd managed to stay warm and interested as long as they were involved but now the supply of leaves in the neighborhood was running low and the men felt like a drink. The little kiddies were getting over-tired and whining to be held; the not so little kiddies were getting bored - *hey - this is Goosey night, isn't it?* The volunteer firemen were getting real specific about where to dump the leaves - *hey you not there!* There was a real big pile growing up on the street between the pool on the north side and the stream that ran under the street and through the properties to the river on the south. Their caution came out of the dry spell the town had been experiencing since early on in September. One of the firemen even started yelling at the young teacher out of state when she tried to organize a leaf fight. This coming on top of the wet candles did the young teacher in - she started crying right there in front of everybody and this so alarmed her 2nd graders that they all started crying too.

The minister's daughter was gnawing on a wart she got from telling lies. That's what her Father called all the things she knew - lies. He said the reason she got warts was for the lies and if she didn't stop telling them, she'd get a good case of leprosy and all her fingers would fall off and that meant no more Girl Scout cookies. The minister's daughter was listening hard for single words to come out at her from across the pool. Her Mother said she had ears like an Indian. Her Mother said she could hear the grass grow. It wasn't true. She'd tried. She heard somebody say *mommy*. She stopped gnawing. Then she heard *goddamn* and some kids crying. She didn't hear what she wanted though - she didn't hear her name called out or *home free all.!!* The water in the pool made certain sounds real clear like music and brakes. She could hear somebody singing *Everyday* from way off.

The minister's daughter shifted her attention to the contractor's wife who was standing underneath the streetlight all by herself watching the people just like the minister's daughter was watching her - in secret. It was like in that cone of yellow light all that ever was - was the contractor's wife. There was no sound there - there was no town - there was no school or playing. The water in the pool was holding still - flat as a shadow still - just like the contractor's wife - just like the minister's daughter. Everything was holding still. That was how it felt. The minister's daughter suddenly felt tired of not ever getting found. She never got found. She was willing to bet all the other kids forgot about her or got mad when they couldn't find her. They all probably just stopped looking. The minister's daughter felt tears - hot and stingy - in her eyes.

The contractor's wife turned in the light towards the pool. The minister's daughter felt like the contractor's wife was seeing her in the dark but she couldn't, *could she?* It was too pitch black inside the shadow of the hill and the contractor's wife was too far. Just to make sure, the minister's daughter waved and then the dark changed and she felt them in there with her - boys. It smelled like boys. The minister's daughter got excited. Somebody had finally come out looking for her. She held still as could be.

"What're ya' doin'?"

"Hey, come 'awn."

Their voices sounded close - almost right beside her but they couldn't be - too fast.

"Chickenshit," was further out across the pool.

"You guys are nuts" was the first voice.

The minister's daughter felt scared - scared for the first time in her life - scared of getting found.

"Crimminy-"

"Wha-at?"

"I can't see-"

"Just come 'awn."

There were lots of them - there were so many boys in the grass with her. And they were all big. The minister's daughter squatted down.

"What was that?"

Silence.

The first voice was the Poole boy who cleared the gutters on the Church House for her Father every Fall; she recognized his voice because he was nice to her sometimes in summer; he let her sit on the dugout when the unions played ball.

"Fuck you."

That was a bad word.

"Fuck you."

Then right in front of her - the black water in the pool plopped. It went - plop. And then another - plop.

"What're ya' doin'?' was the plumber's son.

"Nuthin'" was the Poole boy again.

The minister's daughter knew if she stretched out her hand right now in the dark, she'd feel him. Plop. They were all around her looking - feeling in the dark. Plop. One was right in the front of her - she could just make out an inky blackness darker than the dark. Plop. The minister's daughter was getting too excited. She held her ears and shut her eyes so nothing could get in. Her Father warned her not to get excited. When she got excited, the minister's daughter screamed - no matter where she was - like the time in the 1st grade when the teacher let the students have a relay up and down the aisles in-between the desks and when they tagged her, she screamed and wet her pants and had to wait outside the classroom all by herself until her Mother came and said it didn't matter but it did. She couldn't stand it anymore. The minister's daughter stood up and let go of her ears and listened! They were on the hill behind her, scraping, grunting up - good - she wasn't up there - good - she was down here in the shadow – good - the big boys couldn't find her - good. And then her eyes swam in the yellow cone of light across the pool and the eyes of the contractor's wife surfaced. And then the minister's daughter watched the contractor's wife lift her hand up and wave directly at her and the minister's daughter took a start, but her shoe got stuck and her foot pulled out and she pitched forward off balance into the dark and landed in the black pool - plop.

Two 4th grade boys were almost to the top of the telephone pole and dangerously close to the power lines before one of their mothers saw them. *Get down now,* and *Watch it,* and *Come on* came up at them from below and they would have too but one of their fathers was all red-faced from a couple of beers off the back of the fire truck and was yelling up at them and making them afraid to get down which was why they didn't hear the minister's daughter yell.

Like good timing, the garbageman, a friendly guy who lived off the highway in the woods by himself, arrived with a garbage truckfull of dead leaves and the crowd cheered. He said somebody called him up - sounded like a woman and that he was real glad to get these leaves *offa'* his hands and then somebody - not one of their mothers - said how about getting the 2 kids on the telephone pole to jump into the truckfull of leaves which sounded like a good idea to the crowd who cheered some more.

They were at the top climbing up and over - then on their feet running - all of them - in the dark. Joe Poole's son didn't feel exactly okay about this but *boy oh boy, it was great* - now that they were up here on the property north of Mountain Avenue. He couldn't see *nuthin'* but the distant lick of dark gleam in the windows in the fieldstone house. All they wanted to do was scare her. And then from down below, the people in the town were yelling and he felt like it was the contractor's wife cheering him on.

"Yahoo!" Joe Poole's son waved his hands at the crowd.

"Shut-up!"

Somebody pulled him down. He had the hiccups. He couldn't stop the hiccups. Somebody slapped a can of beer in his hand and he took a long hard tug.

"Help..."

"What was that?"

His cousin was beside him up on his feet. Joe Poole's son stood up too. Down the hill across the pool, the garbage truck was dumping a whole truckfull of dead leaves on the pile. The Fire Chief was going nuts trying to stop it. The mayor was crossing over and so was Chief of Police. There were 2 kids being picked off the telephone pole by the hook and ladder guys. People kept pointing up. And then he saw her. She was in-between the pool and the leaf pile. She was standing there all by herself. Her hair was loose. It seemed to him every time he'd ever seen the contractor's wife, she was standing all by herself.

Headlights blinked on then off. Joe Poole's son was positive he saw it. Then once more. Headlights out across the valley near the river blinked on and off - and not just any headlights.

"Help me!"

The yellow parking light below the main globe on the right was out - wouldn't work no matter what they did. His cousin who was good at things electrical had tried. They'd taken it back up to the dealership but none of their guys could fix the right hand parking light on his Dad's pickup either.

"Help!"

Joe Poole's son looked down at the pool. Somebody was in there. The contractor's wife turned too. She must have heard it. She was looking at the pool. Joe Poole's son watched her light a match. There was a wind picking up. The match went out. Then she must have struck another because her face lit up with orange in the dark. And then he watched her drop the lit match in the pile of leaves.

The minister's daughter couldn't get out of the pool. Her feet were below her in the water - stuck in mud. Her coat was getting wet. She could move but barely and when she did, she seemed to lose her way. In the dark, the edge around the pool wasn't there when she reached for it - no matter which way. She tried to feel for grass - for anything - for ground that was solid - for something to hold onto. A breeze kicked up and pulled across her face and with it came the smell of fire - *where?* She couldn't see a thing but the yellow glare from the streetlight across the pool. It looked so far away - like from another town.

"Mommy."

The water in the pool lapped. She heard it. The breeze was in the pool. She listened hard. Everything was quiet then lapping hills of water purled in her ears. Then rap, snap, knock, click, crack, crackle - fire! In her eyes, a bonfire lit up into the night! It licked the dark with streaks and threw up flying embers that fell like shooting stars. The pool lapped. The water climbed up higher - to her chest.

"Mommy."

The minister's daughter had to get out of here. She looked for help. There was no fire in the pool - no reflected embers - no shooting stars. It was flat black still except for the lapping - she could hear it lapping. The water came up around her neck and touched her chin. And then from deep inside its dark surface, the minister's daughter watched white and flapping wings emerge like migrating birds and then the dark itself began to move - she felt its outflow - moving through her hair - rippling at her mouth. And then hands - huge and powerful hands clamped down on her shoulders and ripped her free.

"No virgin sacrifice - no virgins today."

The minister's daughter wasn't sure she'd heard it. She stood up on the bank to screeching seagulls hovering in the air before her eyes with flames shooting high-up behind them in the night. And she screamed and she screamed.

Joe Poole's son couldn't believe what he **was** seeing. The fireball down below was rocking in the wind. And then the pop of beebee guns sounded in his ears and he turned for the report.

Nothing happened - no sound - no shattered glass. His cousin pulled back on the pump and took dead aim at the fieldstone house. His cousin was a crackshot but still no spitting-hail sound of beebees hitting home. They picked themselves up off their bellies and ran along the lawn until they were within 15 feet of the house.

"What in hell-"

The fieldstone house was flat and dark and still like a shadow. They were shooting beebees into a shadow - that's what he remembered all the rest of his life thinking - shooting beebees into a shadow like whistling in the wind. And then behind them an enormous blast filled the air as the garbage truck exploded and the fire lifted in a great wall of blaze up into the dark.

They watched it for a minute. They all stood there watching it for a minute. And that was something strange too - the fire ball wasn't shining hot at their faces. Joe Poole's son turned to look. There was no orange shine on the lawn or in the little panes of glass in the windows on the house either. It was cool and dark on the hill. Joe Poole's son felt drawn to the fieldstone house. He felt it like a lure - it was in his chest. He felt like he wanted to get as close as he could.

"No. Come 'awn." It was his cousin; he was spooked.

Joe Poole's son shrugged his cousin off. He took a step. The ground underneath his sneaker sank. He looked down. The ground felt like velvet. His cousin let off a stream of beebees - into the ground - into the house. The action of the pump sliding back and forth was the only sound there was.

"Can you friggin' believe this fire?" The plumber's son came up behind them in the dark

"Hey, the ground's soft" was the bricklayer's son.

Poole

He heard it. His cousin heard it. They all heard it.

147

His cousin had his arm. "Ferget it - ya' hear me!"

"Who is that?" The bricklayer's son was backing up.

There was no wind. Joe Poole's son noticed that. There was no wind on her land. It occurred to him the fire wouldn't be coming up the hill.

"Come 'awn - I said." His cousin had him by the shirt.

Their eyes met. He was breathing steady. He felt sure. His cousin let go and took off with the other guys into the dark. And then a draft came up and played around his thighs - working up his chest to his face - and he smelled the contractor's wife - in his teeth. Sweat broke out on his forehead and a great blast of hot air hit him in his face. Then he heard a hiss like air escaping from a tire. He looked up. And the moon came out and lit on a man - dark and short with a great barrel chest. He was on the peak of the slate roof. And he was hissing. A gust carried a spray of dying embers almost to the roof. It fell short and Joe Poole's son felt the heat suck back on a deep breath. The dark man walked with a limp along the peak to the middle and watched the fire. Joe Poole's son turned and watched as a piece of fire broke off and landed on the lawn. The man on the roof filled his chest and hissed. And the fire on the lawn skidded back a few feet.

Joe Poole's son grinned. He felt like nothing could ever get him. The fire lifted up higher over the crest of the hill. It looked like an orange Niagara. His Dad had taken him fishing on a trip up there near the Canadian border last summer - he was 15. His Dad rented a canoe and they went into the wild for a whole week together. They ate what they killed and drank the mountain water. It tasted so good to him. He drank some hard cider his Dad brought along. They had it their last night. It was just the two of them and a small ditch fire - his Dad on one side looking so relaxed and easy. They sucked on birch twigs. Joe Poole's son remembered talking and talking and his Dad just listening.

The dark man was hissing. The orange shine from the fire appeared on the rim of the hill like a horizon. It caught hold and shimmered there for a minute before it slid over on the lawn and the ground sizzled like a bog. A horn was honking. The shine slid around the ground like water seeking level. His Dad said something last summer about a man's responsibility. He could hear a horn honking - it seemed way off. The dark man wasn't on the roof anymore. His Dad said a man did what he had to - what others before him had agreed to. His Dad said the price was autonomy.

Lilacs - Joe Poole's son smelled lilacs. The softest scent of lilacs filled the air. Joe Poole's son liked the scent of lilacs even more than cut grass. It was funny now him thinking of *autonomy*. A hot wind blew up and pushed the scent of lilacs off him.

Poole

Joe Poole's son wondered if this was what his Dad meant. The shine was halfway across the lawn - little orange rivers of shine coming his way. Next to him the softest *click* - softer than a human breath and with it came the sweetest whiff of lilacs. Joe Poole's son turned and watched the window near him open. And then the horn was squawking in his ears and he watched the glare of headlights running at him in the night - and not just any headlights - the yellow parking light below the main globe on the right was out. And he could hear his Dad yelling his name.

Joe Poole lifted his foot off the accelerator, downshifted and braked all at the same time. The fire pounced down on the lawn and scattered - little pockets of fire all over winning. Joe Poole yanked his nephew into place behind the wheel and kicked the driver's door open. He couldn't move fast enough around the front fender. There were fires everywhere and flying embers burning his skin.

The window was pushed back wide enough now to see. Joe Poole's son took a step closer and slid kneedeep into shadow. It was so soft. It was cool and deep. And there she was - whole in the window - like breezin' lace. Her body glowed with pearl and dew - she was a will-o-wisp. Her fingers were dainty on the dark like feathers. She turned her palm and reached for his and he saw that she was seasoned - crackled like the tiny panes of glass in her windows - wintry - gloamy. He looked for her eyes. He needed her eyes.

Joe Poole caught his son squarely on the chin. His fist hit bone. He didn't look for what was in the window. He didn't smell for lilac. He lifted his big boy up onto his back and carried him to the pickup and dropped him on the flatbed. For a second - he only took that second - he looked for all that he could see in his only son's face - then he slammed his fist against the fender and the pickup with his son and his nephew in it roared out across the land -

free

Clouds slid across the night sky like riders heading home. The people out on Mountain Avenue didn't see it coming. Townsmen were trying to close the outflow doors that fed the stream in the hope that the pool would overflow its banks. Trenches were getting dug and brushfires were being set to clear the land. Everybody there was doing their best to contain the fire when the minister's daughter came screaming out of the flames. The mayor caught her in his arms; she was crazy yelling *run run run* when the wind turned. The whole town felt it pause and later said it smelled of lilacs. Then the wind caught in people's hair and at their clothes and pushed them back and the fire followed them across the road. Within seconds, the roof on the town councilman's house on the south side of Mountain Avenue caught fire - then the house next door caught it too. The fire jumped and caught on a tree that shuddered into flame. It was moving fast now that it was loose and on a direct heading for town. People scattered for their cars. The chief told one of his volunteers to call the fire department in the neighboring township for help but he had an awful feeling that it wouldn't do much good.

Thunder banged as the pickup with the broken front light turned onto Post Road and practically flew along the asphalt at him. The chicken farmer watched it skid under 2 streetlights spraying water instead of leaves. The chicken farmer thought that was funny – so much water in the street. When it got to him, the pickup stopped.

"Get in." It was the nephew.

Poole's son was out like a light on the flatbed.

"I ain't waitin for you." It was a warning - the nephew was scared.

The chicken farmer hustled out of his truck into Poole's. As he was doing this, he noticed a slick and steady stream of water running down the street. The nephew didn't wait for him to close the door.

The contractor's babysitter was just 15 - she was watching the cloudbank slide into place. There was water in the wind. It whipped in at her at the door like sand. The kids were sitting on the couch ready. The contractor's wife had called and told her what to pack. The babysitter could see the fire coming now through the properties and it was coming quick like a steamroller smashing down the land. She hoped the contractor's wife would get here soon. The babysitter wanted to go home. She lived with her Mom and her sister over the Beauty Parlor which was where her Mom worked. She hoped her Mom was okay. And then instead of the sky opening up and it raining down - a geyser full of water exploded up into the night. She watched it just keep going - up and up. She could see it in the lightning - she could see it in the moon - out there beyond the properties - out there on Mountain Avenue - water climbing up and up to meet the clouds and then it burst and was a torrent on the fire and the land. And then the dark green Buick pulled in at the curb and the contractor's wife got out.

The babysitter got the children down the path with all of their belongings. She was carrying a big bible-sized book the contractor's wife had told her to get out of a trunk in the garage. The contractor's wife was on the far side of the green Buick watching the geyser put out the fire. She took the book, and placed it in the Buick on the seat. The kids were sitting still in back like they had been on the couch - not a word - not one single word or cry even. The contractor's wife and the babysitter watched the fire get swallowed in a fogbank, then the contractor's wife climbed into the driver's seat and pulled the door closed and the babysitter watched the dark green Buick ride away into the dark. And then the water fell out of the clouds and the babysitter ran home.

There's a lot of different versions that went around about what happened to that suburb in that time but the one that stuck was that the stream that ran out from the pool through the properties to the river acted as a sort of mountain channel and in the space of roughly 10 hours flooded out the town. The people there - the Dutch Reformed and the Catholics - the town council, the Ladies' Society, the Landmark Committee, the Hospital Volunteers - well just about everybody - managed to get out with kith and kin. Some even managed to save family heirlooms and books and childhood treasures. It's funny what people take with them when it comes down to it. All the maple trees drowned. That took a while though. The underground river that had exploded through the bedrock (nobody knew how or why - it was all speculation) just kept coming and eventually the entire valley became a reservoir for the county and even supplied some of the cities along the Hudson. There was only 1 fatality - his name was Joe Poole.

Anybody who has a mind to or a need can still go out there and see where the suburb used to be. It's clear and crystal and in the Fall, black birds and seagulls flock there. It's quite a sight really. The Poole family still lives and works the land on what would have been the river but now of course is an enormous expanse of reservoir. On the far side in the hills, there's a fieldstone house.

NOTES

Summer
Kelly + Erin Bucket List 201

- Bike the island
- Get blonde + tan (obviously)
  ↳ also back of legs

- fish
- str8 chill 😛
- make some healthy + dank lunches
- become UFOBI members
- paddle board sunrise ☀
- water ski

Made in the USA
Charleston, SC
31 October 2011